DEUTSCHLAND

1913–1914

HISTORY OF VON SCHATT

1913–1960

Copyright © 2021, 2023 Richard Daub.
All rights reserved.

Cover design by Richard Daub.

42º6'6.6"N 48º6'6.6"W

No literary agent, corporate editor, unemployed MFA, or anyone affiliated with an educational institution assisted in the writing, publication, or editing of this book.

ISBN: 978-1-946094-05-6

First Edition Paperback, 2023 Clay Road Press

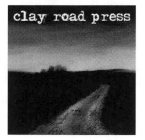

www.richarddaub.com

@rdaub82

The girl had never seen a man so handsome as the one who stepped into Father's Inn on that brisk December afternoon in 1913, and she knew he was her only hope.

Two weeks earlier, she learned that Father — *The Innkeeper*, as he was known in Lüneburg, famous for its salt mines and Bach's organ — had arranged her matrimonial affairs in a cloakroom deal with one of the men from church, whose oldest son, a sweaty, obese boy named Fritz, who sang in the choir and aspired to someday take over the family stationery shop, she was now slated to wed in three months, on her fifteenth birthday, their names already inked in *The St. Johannis Lutheran Day Planner, 1914 Edition*, changes to which were strictly forbidden.

Most of the lodgers were men around Father's age, broken souls draped in tattered suits traveling from town-to-town selling encyclopædias or band instruments or some other such thing nobody wanted — but this one was young, tall, and handsome, clad in a black silk suit, the kind that Father would describe as "Satan's garb". And he wasn't trying to sell anything, enquiring only about the placard hanging in the front window that Father had painted in his workshop:

3

ATTENTION TRAVELERS!
ROOM TO LET!
SINGLE NIGHT RATES!

So suspicious was Father of this traveler that he quoted twice the regular rate for one of the two small guest rooms at the back of the house. But the man did not object or attempt to haggle, saying only, "That would be vonderful, sir."

The young man from Boizenburg signed his name in the guest register as "Christian Schmidt"—an alias his father suggested he use in the rural Christian towns he would be passing through on his way south. While signing the register, he felt the blazing blue eyes of his host scrutinizing his every movement, but he maintained his discipline, and pretended not to notice the girl spying him from atop the stairs, making sure not to look up at her while being shown to his room.

The girl retreated to her quarters, where, at this time of day, she should have been studying her Bible, but instead usually spent hours on the mattress concocting fantasies of handsome travelers rescuing her from this one-horse town. Today, though, she really did retrieve her Good Book and sat at her desk, opening it to the first of several blank pages at the end of *Revelation* following John's warning of God's punishment to anyone who dare add to the prophetic words of this Book, and, with her freshly dipped feathered quill, began writing—

Dear Mister Traveler,

I am being held prisoner by the people who own this house. They are not my real parents. My real parents are

4

dead. Please help me escape. I have been here since I was a little girl. They beat me and treat me like their slave. Please meet me at St. Johannis Church at midnight. I will be hiding in the bushes. I have some marks we can use on the journey. Please tell no one of this.

Signed,
The Imprisoned Maiden

Carefully she tore the page from the book, aware that Father's keen ear could pick up the tearing of scritta all the way downstairs. Then, on the next blank page, she began another letter, this one to her parents, knowing Father would be enraged when he recognized the paper it was written on—

Dear Father and Mother,

I have been made with child by a boy from a prominent family in town, and I am no longer able to hide my shame in public. Therefore, with this letter, I must bid you good-bye forever, as I do not wish to bring shame upon yourselves or the boy's family. Also, I have formally renounced the Church of Luther and have converted to the Roman Catholic Church. I have already been baptized by a Roman Catholic priest. By the time you read this letter, I will have already left for Poland, where I will birth the bastardly child, then send him to the orphanage. Afterwards I will enter a convent and spend the rest of my life as a Roman Catholic nun, atoning for my sins, and for being born Lutheran.

Signed,

Your Former Daughter

By 9:30 that evening, long after the residents of Lüneburg had turned in, the girl, feeling her freedom within reach, could stay in the house no longer. With letters in hand and pillowcase stuffed with meager belongings and extra undergarments, she slipped out of her room and descended the stairs, being careful not to step on the creaky spots.

Downstairs, she left the letter to her parents on the dining room table and slid the other into the candlelit gap beneath the guest room door. She listened outside the room until she heard the crinkle of scritta, then slipped out to the cold, silent Lüneburg night.

At St. Johannis, she went around back to a utility door that was never locked, planning to shelter herself just inside until it was time to hide in the bushes. The old building, a prime example of classic northern German brick architecture, had originally been constructed as a Catholic church in the 1300s, still a couple of centuries prior to Professor Luther indulging his theses on the door of Wittenburg Castle and prompting the phrase *"Go Lutheran!"* to begin appearing on shop window placards and rear bumpers of horse-drawn wagons all over *Deutschland*. The most striking feature of the church was the steeple that soared 108 meters above the town, the largest steeple in Lower Saxony, but it had a slight lean to it. Local legend told that the master builder noticed his error only after the structure was fully erect, at which point he became so distraught that he ran up the steeple steps and leaped out a window—a fall that surely would have killed him, had not a hay wagon been passing on the thoroughfare below. After recovering from the initial shock of still being alive, the builder interpreted his soft landing as a sign of forgiveness from God, and so overjoyed was he that he decided to celebrate at *Die Gepunktete Amphibie*—The Spotted Amphibian, a popular local tavern of the day, back when there was still a vestige of nightlife in Lüneburg—and drank himself into such a stupor that he fell backwards off a bench and split his head open on the stone hearth, dying moments later to the sound of sizzling blood.

"Have I wandered into a den of monsters?" the young traveler wondered aloud after reading the letter that had materialized on the floor, written on what appeared to be Bible paper—a horrifying thought, until it occurred to him that, this being a Christian town, it was likely torn from a New Testament. After reviewing the day's events—from the stern look the Innkeeper gave him with his blazing blue eyes, to the rather high rate he quoted for such a quaint room, to the letter he now beheld written by the girl at the top of the stairs—he concluded that this Inn was indeed a den of monsters, and that he should help her escape.

It also began to dawn on him that maybe his father had been right. He had always questioned the old man's dire warnings of the evil that continues to linger in the soul of man, even now, 2,600 years after the *Tfutza*, when the Jews were forced from their ancestral homeland, and how, to this very day, they were still being persecuted as they wandered through a world in which they had no home—which never made sense to the boy, as Boizenburg had always been his home, and his neighbors had always been nice to him, and, just three days ago, they had thrown him a farewell sausage fest. They knew him as the boy who liked dysfunctional clocks, and they knew not to throw away their busted chronikers, but instead to bring them to the boy, who would take them to the little workshop his father had set up for him in the barn and disassemble it, cataloguing every piece and building a vast inventory of parts from which he would construct masterful Frankensteinian timepieces. The kid was some kind of eccentric genius, the elders said, though his peers thought he was queer and mostly avoided him. It was a hobby that evolved into a passion during his early teens, and, one day, he approached his father and said he had something important to tell him. The father half-expected his son to tell him he was one of those boys who didn't like girls, but instead he came out as a horologist—a relief, at first, to the old man, until he had a moment to digest it, then rolled his eyes and said *"oy vey"*—but he did have to admit that the kid had genuine talent, so he might as well pursue it to the highest level—which is why he was now on his way to Eisenbach in the Black Forest, chasing the legacy of legendary clockmaker Johann Baptist Beha, son of master clockmaker Vinzenz Beha, best remembered for his shield cuckoo clocks, for which the young man had a particular passion. There he would learn from the best in the world and become a master, and maybe someday clocks with his own name on them would demand a premium from aficionados all over Europe.

Unsettling as it was to have encountered, in the Innkeeper, the very darkness Father had warned of, he had no regrets about disregarding his advice to take the train directly to the Black Forest to get there quickly and avoid unnecessary encounters with the gentiles. He had long dreamed of making this journey and wanted to enjoy it by visiting the clock shops in the villages he passed through, and by taking in the sights and sounds and smells of the countryside while he still could, figuring that, as soon as he secured an apprenticeship, he would be cooped up in a dusty shop for most of his waking hours and rarely get to see the light of day. Yet, he had not envisioned meeting a damsel in distress, not after his disappointing adolescence, when not a girl in Boizenburg, not even the homely ones, would give him the time of day. His mind reconstructed what it could of the blurry peripheral at the top of the stairs, which was enough to convince him that she was beautiful, and, after several more readings of the letter, he had become endeared to her unruly penmanship, and was in love—

Blinded as he was by this unexpected excitement, he knew he must be cautious, as the Innkeeper would surely come looking for the girl as soon as he discovered her gone, and would likely murder him if he was caught with her. However, the young man had another hobby that originated even before his interest in clocks—collecting the printed timetable pamphlets at the Boizenburg train station, which had long been a stop on the Berlin-Hamburg line, where, in the ticket office, there was a big wooden display stand with the timetables for various regional routes, all free for the taking— though Father only allowed him to take one of each. The smell of ink on paper made the boy pleasantly lightheaded, and the rows and columns of printed times—*12:57 1:03 1:19 1:37 1:59 2:13*—were what sparked his initial interest in horology. When he was little, Father used to take him to the station on Sundays to watch the trains come and go, and the boy would log them in his pocket journal with his impeccable handwriting, noting the arrival times and checking them against the timetables. Amazingly, they were almost always exactly on time, which the boy credited to the same German precision and engineering responsible for the printing of the timetable pamphlets themselves, much thanks to Johannes Gensfleisch zur Laden zum Gutenberg and his movable-type printing press. Thus, it was because of this still-active hobby that the young man knew that a southbound train destined for Hanover would be stopping in Lüneburg at 4:37 am, and would be long gone by the time the girl's parents realized she was no longer there.

He waited until the minute hand on his pocket watch struck 11:57—a departure time he calculated would get him to the St. Johannis bushes right on time—before quietly tiptoeing down the hall and out of the house. He arrived at exactly midnight, where the bushes were a-rustle—

"Is that you in there?" he called, quietly.

"It is me," said the girl, springing upright. "Follow me. I know where there is an open door. We will be safer inside."

He followed her around back, then through a utility door. Inside, she took his hand and led him through a maze of dark corridors that led to the main cathedral illumined by the 99 white luft candles lit by the altar boys every evening at sunset. He had never seen the inside of a church and was astounded at how lavish it was—baroque figurines, stained-glass curtains, fancy candles, and, up on the second level at the back of the cathedral, Lüneburg's marquee tourist attraction, the great organ that, two centuries prior, Johann Sebastian practiced on, which, like the steeple hovering askance over town, oozed Christian grandeur and dominance—whereas his own temple back home was a rectangular one-story brick building furnished with three rows of wooden chairs facing a splintered pulpit and an accordion in the corner that hadn't been taken out of its case in seven years.

As beautiful as this place was, it paled to the beauty of the damsel's face, which he now finally had opportunity to behold in the candlelight. He followed her up the aisle to the last pew, just below the majestic organ, where she stopped and kissed him. He had never kissed a girl and was unfamiliar with the nuances of the French tongue-style, prompting her to giggle. She giggled again when his erection rubbed against her thigh, and it felt big, considerably bigger than Father's. Deftly, she undid his trousers, then pulled them down along with his undergarments, only to gasp when she saw that the tip of his thing looked like the head of a mushroom—

The young man had no idea why she gasped, but he was powerless to ask why as she pulled him down to the pew—

"I have never done that before," he said afterwards, his head resting upon her bare bosom as she gently stroked his hair.

"Me neither," she lied. "But it felt vonderful. Was it vonderful for you?"

"Yes, of course," he said. "It was vonderful."

"My whole life they have tried to beat it into me that *this* place was the House of my Savior, but I have always known that this is not true. You are my savior, and it is you who will take me from this dark hellhole forever!"

"But how did you become their prisoner?"

"It is a long story," she said, then told a harrowing tale of how her real mother had died while birthing her, and how her real father was killed in a gruesome salt mine accident, and how she was adopted by the Innkeeper and his wife, who turned her into their personal slave and would beat her if she didn't do her chores and Bible study. She also told him about the man from the church who had made a down payment to the Innkeeper for her to be the bride of his corpulent sweat-soaked son—

"Monsters!" the young man exclaimed, bolting upright. "But never fear, my love, I will take you from this dark hellhole, to the Black Forest!"

11

⚓ ⚓ ⚓

Three days and several lengthy rail station layovers later, the lovers pulled into Donaueschingen station in the dead of night, at the end of the Black Forest Railway, which was the closest they could get to tiny Eisenbach by train. They slept on the depot benches until dawn, then set out in a horse-drawn carriage-cab for the ten-mile journey west to their final destination. Within an hour of their arrival, they located an apartment to rent, the smallest available in town, but with the modern convenience of indoor plumbing—only to be told by the landlord that they would have to pay six months' rent up front since the young man did not yet have secure employment, and that they would also have to produce a marriage certificate, as he did not let his apartments to sinners. So the young couple headed down to the town hall, where the *oberbürgermeister* pronounced them man and wife and presented them with a notarized certificate of marriage that they brought back to the landlord, and the lease was signed.

The young man's next move had been planned for more than half his life—to set out and find a clock shop with the name 'Beha' on it—which he was able to do within minutes, only to have the door slammed in his face by what appeared to be a dogman—creatures, he had read somewhere, known to dwell in the Black Forest, some of whom were fine clockmakers and chocolatiers.

Undeterred by the rejection, which he knew all along might happen, he set out to the other clock shop in town, *der Uhrenladen*, but the lights were off and nobody was home, and it appeared as if no one had been there in quite some time.

For the next several hours, he navigated up and down the *Hauptstraße* hoping to find a shop that he had somehow

12

missed the first dozen times he walked by, until his feet were blistered and the residents were peeking through their curtains. Finally he could walk no more and went into the *gasthaus* to find out if there were any other clock shops in the area—

"Go to Triberg, ten miles to the north," the Innkeeper said. "It is bigger than Eisenbach, and there is more opportunity there. Here you have Beha, and he frightens away the other clockmakers. They all go up there."

After their first night together in the new apartment— during which his new bride had done something with her mouth he had previously never conceived of, then allowed him to put his thing in a place he never would have imagined—the young man, brimming with *fahrvergnügen,* set out the next morning and hired a carriage-cab to Triberg, where he marched into the first clock shop he encountered— Zeitmacher's Haus of Clocks—and secured an apprenticeship. Unfortunately, at age 73 and from the old school, Zeitmacher was interested only in big clocks, and didn't fiddle around with little shield cuckoos—which, for now, was fine with the young man, relieved to at least have some skin in the game after the rough start. Two weeks later, though, it was clear that old man Zeitmacher was himself cuckoo, and that he wasn't going to learn anything here, as all he'd done thus far was mind the store while the old man took naps and sat on the toilet. So he started using his lunch breaks to explore the rest of Triberg, until one day he walked into Alöbärr Schaeffer's Cuckoos, a larger and more professional shop with an odd perfumy smell that gave him an embarrassing erection. It just so happened that Schaeffer was looking to expand further into shield cuckoos and offered him an apprenticeship on the condition that he first work as seasonal help in the store through the Christmas shopping season, then, after the holidays were over, he would turn his attention to teaching the young man everything he knew about shield cuckoos, and, if all worked out, offer him a paid full-time position.

At first, working for Schaeffer was exciting. Although he wasn't being paid, the young man felt like he was finally on the right track. Every evening, before commuting by carriage-cab back to Eisenbach, he would stop at one of the chocolatier shops, enjoying the communal warmth of holiday shoppers just in from the cold, and buy a treat, the least expensive item in the store, for his beloved, whom they would soon learn was with child, due at the end of the summer.

As promised, Schaeffer taught him everything he knew about shield cuckoos. And Schaeffer was impressed by the talent of this kid from the north country, who, in a way, reminded the veteran clockmaker of himself way back when, an outcast merely trying to go quietly about his business in this cruel society of humankind.

"Precision!" he would exclaim, pounding his fist on the workbench, prompting the tiny clock parts to jump. "It matters not how pretty the instrument if it does not tell time precisely!"

Aside from these outbursts, things went swimmingly through the spring of 1914, so it seemed to the apprentice, confident that, any day now, Schaeffer would offer him the paid position, especially with summer fast approaching, when preparations began in earnest for the upcoming Christmas shopping season. He was hoping to avoid asking about it, but his savings were running precariously low, and the child was due in a few short months—

Meanwhile, in the Balkans—now commonly being

referred to in the papers as "the powder keg of Europe", where fighting had been going on for a couple of years now — tensions, much thanks to Russian meddling, had been escalating, prompting the powers-that-be in Europe to bulk up their militaries, including the Bavarians, who were getting desperate in their efforts to keep pace and were now recruiting outside their traditional jurisdictions, including Triberg, where they had opened an ancillary recruiting office and posted silkscreened placards all over town:

THE BAVARIAN ARMY WANTS YOU!
YES, YOU!
PAID SERVICE UPON ENLISTMENT!
RUN TO RECRUITING OFFICE NOW!
FREE CIGARETTES!
RUN!

The young apprentice, though, paid little attention to the placards, or anything else, so focused was he on honing his craft and further impressing Schaeffer that he would have no choice but to finally offer him the paid position —

On the 28th of June, an otherwise splendid summer Sunday in Sarajevo, the Archduke Franz Ferdinand, heir presumptive to the Austro-Hungarian throne and owner of a handlebar mustache that made women faint in the streets, was taken out, prompting The July Crisis, when the nations of Europe tried to show each other who had the biggest *schwanz*. While everyone else in the Black Forest, including the cows, pigs, dogs, and sheep, heard the gongs of war to the east, all the aspiring horologist heard was ticking —

"Any day now," he would sigh, unaware that Schaeffer was not actually preparing for the Christmas retail season, but getting ready to flee to his farm near Pfalzgrafenweiler, where he had already stashed his most valuable inventory of clocks and love potions in places where invading soldiers would never find them, and where he planned to live in the guise of a peasant beet farmer until this shitstorm blew over. Yet, so oblivious was the apprentice—even when there were only a few clocks left in the store, the really ugly ones no one would ever buy—that it was an utter shock when, one morning in late July, he showed up for work and found a placard on the door painted in Schaeffer's hand announcing that the shop had gone out of business forever.

Heart pounding, the young apprentice searched for his mentor, but many of the other shops in town had also shuttered, and the owners of the ones still open seemed unusually paranoid and claimed to have no idea where he or any of the others had gone. Savings nearly gone, he began roaming the streets of Triberg looking for any kind of work, enquiring about cashier positions at the stationery shop and the *Acht-Fünf*—the Eight-Five, a corner convenience store—but no one was hiring.

By August—when Germany declared war on Russia, then, two days later, on France, and then the Brits declared war on Germany—the only place in town still open was the Bavarian Army recruiting office. Even now he had yet to tell his wife about losing the apprenticeship, and that they no longer had a *pfennig* to their name. The dream gone and the child due any day now, the young man stood in the steamy late-summer rain staring at the placards until the cuckoos directed him to the warm glow of the recruiting office up the street. He started running towards it, slow at first, then sprinting—

⚓ ⚓ ⚓

Another late summer storm pounding Munich had turned the *exerzierplatz* training field into a muddy soup, prompting Drill Sergeant Milhaüs Meisterjäger to move the day's scheduled marching exercises inside the mess hall in order not to have to endure a second consecutive day of sitting down to supper with a cold, wet uniform clinging to his aching body and his fingertips shriveled like prunes.

As if the weather weren't enough, his beloved Bavarian Army had, of late, been signing up anyone it could find— including the daydreaming clockmaker and the creepy Austro-Hungarian watercolorist—and it was his job to turn this ragtag regiment of misfits into a tight unit of killing machines. Accepting the clockmaker was one thing—at least he was *Deutsche*, and at least he was kind of trying—but accepting this screwball painter that his own country's army rejected was a new low, and who, last night, on the food service queue, became enraged when the clockmaker held up the line to ask the cook if he knew how to make potato latkes—

"They do not serve Jew food in the Bavarian Army!" the watercolorist exclaimed.

In disbelief, the clockmaker turned to him and said, "They are potato pancakes. 'Latkes', 'potato pancakes'—whatever you wish to call them, they are quite delicious. Have you ever tried them?"

"I do not eat Jew food!"

"For the love of Moses, they are potatoes! Everyone eats potatoes!"

"Inferior Jew!"

Meisterjäger, having just sat down and about to take his

first bite of sausage, had to get up in his wet uniform and separate the two men before they came to blows. He considered letting them have at it to get it out of their systems, but, with everyone sitting down to eat, it didn't seem the appropriate moment. Then, today, during the marching drill in the mess hall—a bit of a tight space, the old drill sergeant knew, for such an exercise—the clockmaker and the watercolorist were struggling to bear their arms, which were not supposed to be loaded during this early stage of training, when the clockmaker accidentally swatted the watercolorist in the chin with the butt of his rifle—

The clockmaker turned to apologize, but found himself staring at the business end of a Luger inches from his forehead. There was a flash and a pop, and a spray of blood against the concrete wall behind him. His suddenly lifeless body collapsed to the floor, his head settling into an expanding pool of blood on the highly-buffed black linoleum—

"Hitler, you imbecile!" Meisterjäger roared.

"I acted in self-defense, sir," said the watercolorist, coldly.

⚓   ⚓   ⚓

Not only had the girl been experiencing the usual discomforts of being with child—her size, in particular, making it difficult to sleep and use the toilet—she had, of late, been feeling sharp, hot cramps, as if her uterus were being jabbed by a hot poker.

One night, towards the end of August, in addition to the hot pokers, she started feeling dull aches every couple of minutes. She sweated it out until her midwife, Blagorodna—a short, stout, teakettle-shaped Bulgarian woman with a ladystache and armpits that smelled of onion, who spoke no *Deutsche*—arrived in the morning and delivered a baby boy—

"*Dyavola!*" she gasped, dropping the child on his mother and scurrying out the door, reciting *The Lord's Prayer* in Bulgarian as she nearly took out the military officer in the hallway—

Turning the corner from the staircase on the second-floor corridor of the ramshackle apartment house, Sergeant Milhaüs Meisterjäger was nearly barreled over by a short mustachioed woman mumbling something in a foreign tongue, but managed to step aside to allow her by. He then proceeded towards the open door at the end of the hall, picking up a foul odor as he neared, and stopped at the doorway, where he took a moment to digest the sight of the girl and the bloody infant child on the bed—

"Err, madam," he said quietly, hat in hand. "Pardon the interruption, but I bear important news. May I come in?"

The girl, drenched with sweat, looking towards him but seemingly unaware of his presence, did not answer. The child, though, was looking right at him with eyes like blue fire—

"Madam," he said, stepping inside and gently closing the door. "There has been an accident at the *exerzierplatz*. Your husband, I am sorry to inform you, has passed. My deepest condolences."

The girl did not move.

"Madam, did you hear what I have said?"

"I heard," she said.

"Do you need help, madam? Are you hurt?"

"I am fine."

"Are you here alone?"

"Yes."

He looked around the room, then back at the girl. He did

not know if she was really fine or if he should summon help.

"Do you understand what I have told you?"

"Yes."

"Do you have someone to take care of you?"

"No."

"No family? Your Father and Mother?"

"They are dead. I have no family now, except the child."

"Madam, with *Deutschland* at war, you are not safe here alone. Is there nowhere else you can go?"

"No."

"Do you have money?"

"No."

He did not want to leave her alone, but it had been a three-hour train ride out here to fulfill his duty of personally delivering the news of her husband's death, and, as much as he wanted to help, it was imperative he not miss the next train back to Munich—

"Here," he said, pulling a wad of *papiermarks* from his trousers pocket and offering it to her, but she did not take it. "Go north to one of the Scandinavian countries. Sweden, I recommend—beautiful cities and countryside, and the Swedish people are kind and well-attired. Take a train north and then get on a boat—but do not go through Hamburg— leave instead from Bremerhaven. It is a smaller port, which will be safer. If the authorities in Sweden stop you, tell them you are a war refugee from *Deutschland*. But you must get cleaned up and go now. Nowhere in *Deutschland* is safe, especially out here alone in this dark forest."

Finally she looked at the marks, then took them.

"*Danke*," she said.

When the man had gone, the girl pushed herself off the bed and wrapped the child in the sheet. She brought him into the bathroom and drew a shallow bath, washing him until his skin was pink and clean. She bundled him in a towel and placed him on the floor, while she emptied the tub and drew a clean bath for herself. Afterwards, she sat on the toilet seat and fed him.

An hour later, mother and child were in a carriage-cab on their way to Donaueschingen station, where they boarded the evening train north. She briefly felt exhilarated at fleeing the apartment prison she had been trapped in for the past nine months, but exhaustion soon set in, made worse by the near-impossibility of getting any real sleep in the uncomfortable old rail cars.

She was feverish by the time they arrived in Offenburg, where she twice fed the boy in the public toilet during the six-hour layover. Next they boarded a train to Frankfurt, a leg that took six hours instead of the scheduled four due to a breakdown just outside Baden-Baden. After another public toilet feeding, they boarded a train to Hannover, and her fever continued to rise. At one point, passing through a small village, she saw, out the window, old man Heinrich von Schatt from Lüneburg standing at the crossing, with his shock of white hair and long white beard, wearing the same soiled red and white suit he was wearing when she was five and witnessed him urinating on St. Johannis Church, brick wall steaming in the winter air, the old man coming down hard in the harsh Sunday morning sunlight. Then she saw him again in the next village, and the next one, and every one they passed through for the next six hours. At Hannover, she fed the boy again, then they boarded a train to Bremen, on which she slept for the entire three hour leg—which the boy did not mind, swaddled in Mother's arms, staring up at the black window, not knowing what he was looking at, but understanding that they were in motion and headed north.

At Bremen station, they hurried across the platform to catch the 3:45 am to Bremerhaven, the last leg of the journey. The old man again started appearing out the window, and she believed that God was punishing her, and that He had cursed her child, who was making her ill, and would kill her if she didn't get rid of it soon—

When the conductor came through, he punched her ticket and offered it back, but she did not take it, instead asking if he could be so kind as to write a name on the back of it for her—

The conductor was happy to oblige, retrieving from his breast pocket the little pencil he used for crossword puzzles— a recent craze among *Deutsche* railroad conductors—and, leaning against the top of the seat in front of her, wrote neatly on the blank side of the ticket the name she told him, spelling out the last name—*Heinrich von Schatt*—then handed it back to her, smiling—

On the platform in Bremerhaven, child in arms, pillowcase dangling at her side, sky changing from black to blue, North Sea air damp and salty, she had no idea where to go, until the boy cooed. She looked into his blazing blue eyes and started walking west, towards the sea, then north on the ankle-twisting cobblestones of the *Barkhausenstraße*, across the harbor from the freight piers, until arriving at a bend where there was an old brick building with caged windows. Above the main entrance was a tattered green awning with faded white lettering—

SISTERS OF MERCY ORPHANAGE
BREMERHAVEN ANCILLARY LOCATION

On the shadowed steps beneath the awning, mother fed

child one last time. When her breasts were depleted, she slid the train ticket into the towel he was wrapped in, then placed him in front of the door. Without looking back, she proceeded up the *Franziusstraße*, until arriving at a freight pier where no one was around. She wandered through the cargo hold door of a docked steam freighter to a corner behind a stack of shipping crates, where she fell unconscious—

It would be nearly three weeks before her decomposing body would be discovered in the hold of the freighter during unloading in the New York City borough of Brooklyn. Captain and crew could only guess where she had come from, there having been several stops before Bremerhaven, and one afterwards, in Southampton, England. After the body went unclaimed in the city morgue, it was shipped to Hart Island in the Bronx, where the city's unclaimed dead had been buried since the Civil War.

BREMERHAVEN

1919-1936

To an outside observer, five-year-old Heinrich von Schatt could have appeared the model orphan—a tall, strapping boy with thick blond hair and bright blue eyes, who always followed directions and was never insubordinate, and who possessed healthy doses of the prized German principles of order, discipline, and precision—yet, the Ancillary Sisters, widely regarded as some of the cruelest nuns in a land known for tough mothers, feared him, as did the other orphans, so much so that they converted one of the storage rooms in the building's Isolated Wing into his "quarters". Thus, he was the only orphan to have his own space, while, in the main wing, they were squeezing in three, four, five to a room, depending on season.

In his quarters, there were two large windows that, through the exterior cage, provided sweeping views of the shipping piers across the harbor. At all hours he would spot the arriving and departing ships through his seaman's spyglass and record them in his log, impeccably writing the date, time, and ship type. He submerged himself in old books, poring over ocean maps and charts, admiring the illustrations and paintings of great seafaring vessels, reading anything he could find about the RMS *Titanic* and Captain Edward John Smith. He was particularly interested in the coordinates reported by *Titanic* Senior Wireless Operator Jack Phillips in the CQD distress calls transmitted on that fateful night seven years earlier—*41.44 N 50.24 W*, then, ten minutes later, *41.46 N 50.14 W*, seven miles away—

Heinrich's favorite map—one included in a tattered copy of *Werner's Collected Maps and Charts of the World Seas, Third Edition* (1879), which he found in the orphanage library and never returned—had handwritten depth measurements of the North Atlantic and crudely drawn outlines of the Grand Banks of Newfoundland, the shallow, cod-rich waters about 1,200 miles east-northeast of New York that, to the south and east, precipitously dropped from 300 to 15,000 feet, to the Sohm Abyssal Plain and Newfoundland Ridge, and, to the east, the Newfoundland Basin, where SWO Phillips transmitted the CQDs. On one particular map, the southeast corner of the Grand Banks was shaped like an arrowhead pointing directly at an "X" that Heinrich estimated to be at *42°6'6.6"N 48°6'6.6"W*. He'd seen X's on other maps in the same general area, but there were never any references to what was there, just question marks written by the previous owner of the maps. Smith and other Captains of the period must have seen these same maps in *Werner's* and elsewhere, and few are the Captains who can resist the lure of an "X" on an old map. He suspected that Smith, who knew White Star Line was planning on getting rid of him, was worried that the *Titanic* crossing was his last chance to see what, if anything, was at the "X", and why he was willing to risk navigating into an area where sightings of ice fields had been reported—

Shortly after his fifth birthday, Heinrich began attending kindergarten at St. Arnold's, the Catholic schoolhouse around the block on *Bürgermeister-Smidt-Straße*, named after St. Arnold of Soissons, the patron saint of hop-picking brewers and, most recently, steamers of Hamburg sandwiches. Because the children were so afraid of him—his mere presence distracted them to utter dysfunction—the teacher-nuns put his desk out in the corridor, just outside the classroom door where he could hear the teacher, but where the teacher and other children could not see him—though they always knew he was there, as lessons were hardly ever interrupted by the raised hand of a child asking to use the potty, which would have necessitated walking past his desk in the hall. Heinrich, though, did not mind, believing that the teacher-nuns were accommodating him, so that he would not have to endure the other children.

Then one foggy Christmas Eve, 1919, all of the Ancillary orphans, save Heinrich, were in the common room warming their hopeful souls with their annual cup of hot cocoa, when they were further tickled a-titter by the arrival of jolly Mr. Becker—the raspy-voiced local benefactor who showed up each Christmas Eve bearing gifts for the orphans, who looked like a circus ringmaster with his slick black hair and thin handlebar mustache, clad in shiny black silk suit with provocatively high red collar and matching black and red gentleman's cape, his soles sparking low in smart high-heeled boots. Last year, each orphan received a new pair of socks, and, the year prior, mittens—but, this year, seeing how heavy the box appeared in Mr. Becker's arms as he set it on the table, they knew inside must be something special—

"What's in the box?" asked six-year-old Heidi, the sweet, blond-haired girl with the pigtails who was born without hands, and heartbroken the year they got the mittens—

"Why, Heidi, it's so good to see you," said Mr. Becker, grinning. "Have you thought about what we discussed last time? As you know, madness is like gravity... Oh, never mind, we'll talk later. But you wanted to know what's in the box—does anyone else want to know what's in the box?"

The orphans went wild.

"Yeah, we want to know, we want to know," shouted they, gleefully.

"Ask and you shall receive!" said Mr. Becker, snapping his fingers like a magician, the box disappearing in a puff of smoke. When the air cleared, in place of the box, was a new 29 volume set of *Encyclopædia Britannica, Eleventh English Language Edition*—

"Holy smokes!" Sister Clarabell gasped. "A new set of English language encyclopædias for *das waisenhaus*!"

The room erupted in cheers, including Mr. Becker, cheering with them—

"We'll set them in the library tomorrow," said Sister Johanna. "Mr. Becker, this is a generous gift. As always, thank you, and God Bless us, everyone."

"On that note, I must bid *adieu*," he said, snapping and disappearing in a puff of smoke—

In his quarters, Heinrich was looking out the window with his spyglass, but was having difficulty seeing the piers through the fog. Above the horizon, though, he spied something odd, a tiny red glow slowly arcing across the sky. He was then irritated by yet another knock on the door, the second this evening—earlier, Sister Johanna had disturbed him with an invitation for hot cocoa, which, per usual, he declined, in order to continue his work—

"Enter," said Heinrich, annoyed.

The door opened with a puff of smoke, through which appeared Mr. Becker donned in gay apparel—

"Merry Christmas, Heinrich!" he said, festively.

"Are you here to deliver socks?" Heinrich asked.

"No, my young ward."

"I am not your ward."

"So you say."

"State your business."

"To make all of your dreams come true."

"You are wasting my time."

"If I recall correctly, young Heinrich, you want to be a ship Captain when you grow up... do I have that right?"

"This is correct. Now you must vacate my quarters so I can get back to my work."

"I can make it happen."

The boy, blue eyes ablaze, did not respond—

"Yass," Mr. Becker hissed. "It's true. I can make it happen. But wait—do you hear what I hear?"

Heinrich's keen ear picked up orphans cheering in a distant part of the building—

"Do you know why they're cheering?" Mr. Becker asked.

"They have just received new mittens."

"Oh, Heinrich, you slay me. The little bastards are cheering because I just gave them a brand new set of *Encyclopædia Britannica*, fully loaded with maps and charts and ships and biographies of famous Captains and everything you ever wanted to know about the sea—"

Heinrich shifted to conceal the movement in his undergarments—

"Yass, Heinrich, yass," hissed Mr. Becker. "All those maps and ships—but wait, there's more! An entire section devoted to the *Titanic*, with new, never before seen full-color artist renderings of the great disaster. With these books, you will be well on your way to becoming the great ship Captain you long to be—oh, but wait, you'll probably have to put your name on the orphanage library signup list and wait your turn, as there are only 29 volumes, and, oh, so many orphans—"

"I want the *encyclopædias*," Heinrich said.

"Yass, Heinrich, yass, I know you do. But are you willing to pay my asking price to make them yours?"

"I possess only a few marks."

"Oh, silly Heinrich, I don't want your money. But, my boy, this is your lucky day, as all I really need is one little signature on one little piece of parchment, and, *voilà*! They'll be yours for the taking. It'll take no more than two seconds, then I'll be on my way, and you can get back to your work. It really is an awfully simple operation."

In the common room, the orphans, enjoying their biannual Christmas sugar plums and speaking excitedly of all the things they would look up in their new encyclopædias, gasped when Heinrich walked in. They and the sister-nuns watched in horror as he went straight for the *Britannicas*, gathering the first five volumes in his arms and transporting them to his quarters, then, over several trips, the rest of them, until the table was bare.

Sister Clarabell and Sister Johanna knew they were powerless to stop him.

"We are sorry, children," said Sister Clarabell, nearly in tears. "It is all part of God's plan."

"Don't weep, Sister Clarabell," said Heidi. "The dark child may have the encyclopædias, but we still have each other. God bless us, everyone."

⚓   ⚓   ⚓

During Heinrich's seventh year, the Ancillary Sisters invited Captain Jonas Grumbykeiser III, the colorful skipper of the *SMS Elritze*, owned by Howell Freight Lines, which ran several international routes out of Bremerhaven, to speak to the orphans. The Sisters, knowing this was a guest whom Heinrich would want to see, but not wanting to frighten the other orphans, arranged for the Captain to make a private visit to the boy's quarters prior to greeting everyone else in the common room.

Captain Grumbykeiser arrived with a big smile and bearing gifts in the form of old ferry timetable pamphlets he had stumbled upon while nipping *Höhler Whesskey* in the storage room at the ferry-ship office before heading over —

"Thank you, sir," Heinrich said after being handed a dozen timetables for the various Howell cargo routes, his eyes widening at the columns of departure and arrival times. "Do you have more?"

"More? You want more?"

"Yes, sir."

"And what are you going to do with all these old timetables?"

"I plan to be a Captain myself, sir."

"A Captain, aye?"

"Yes, sir."

"Well, blow me down! What is your name, little buddy?"

"Heinrich von Schatt, sir."

"Aye, Captain von Schatt. 'Tis a fine name for a Captain. I'm sure someday you will make a fine seaman, argh."

In the ensuing months, Heinrich started receiving boxes of discarded nautical paperwork—timetables, passenger lists, cargo manifests, advertising brochures, all of which he devoured. Then the shipments suddenly stopped, Heinrich later learning that the *Elritze* had wrecked in the North Atlantic, only a few miles from the coordinates —

⚓   ⚓   ⚓

At age thirteen, Heinrich—six-foot-one, lean, handsome, blinders facing the sea, mast at full staff—attended his final day at St. Arnold's, having reached the age when German boys were no longer required to attend school, and received his diploma from Father Dieter. Afterwards, he returned to his quarters at the orphanage for the last time and retrieved his spyglass and shipping logs, and the pillowcase in which he had packed a spare set of clothing and his shaving razors. At the doorway, he paused to look at all he was leaving behind— the *Encyclopædia*s, the timetables, the shipping paperwork, maps all over the wall—then pivoted a perfect 180° on the ball of his right foot and navigated the long Isolated Wing corridor to the front desk, where Sister Christian officially signed him out, and he was no longer an orphaned child, but a free man—

Watching from her window, Sister Johanna, who'd been waiting thirteen years for this day, crossed herself when she saw him step onto the cobblestones with his belongings and pivot towards the piers. After he'd disappeared from view, she ordered the other Sisters to begin hauling everything from his quarters, including *Encyclopædia*s, down to the furnace. At midnight, after the room had been cleared and scrubbed, there would be an exorcism, followed by a mixer with Father Dieter and the staff from St. Arnold's, where they would dine on steamed Hamburg sandwiches with catsup and Father's homebrew, consuming it until just before dawn, when the dogmen would begin to howl—

The local Captains and deckhands knew Heinrich by sight, having for years seen him watching them through his spyglass—which, as uncomfortable to the superstitious seamen as it was being spied on by the progeny of Satan, was fine, as long as he kept his distance and didn't step foot on the pier. Today, though, he did not have spyglass in hand, and instead navigated past his usual post, then pivoted straight towards them, prompting a frenzy of running up gangways and battening down hatches—

The only sailors in his path who didn't flee were the trio of begrimed and toothless deckhands from *die Eiserne Jungfrau* — the *Iron Maiden*, a ramshackle 200-foot steam freighter down at the far end of the pier—who continued loading their contraband, noticing the lad only when he stopped and saluted them, which initially confused, then humored, the cod-witted pus turds, none of whom had ever been saluted —

It took Heinrich a minute to realize his salute would go unrequited —

"Excuse me," he finally said. "Is Captain Hosenpinkel on board?"

Up in the Wheelhouse, Captain Gerhard Hosenpinkel's lone remaining ear perked up at hearing a new voice and unfamiliar footsteps down below. The old coxswain, now not much more than a skeleton draped in a coat of alcohol-shriveled skin, was seated on the floor, back against helm, legs splayed before him, bottle of *Höhler Whesskey* in hand with only a couple of swigs remaining, long white beard sprouting wildly from ashen face and resting upon unbuttoned coal-smeared Captain's Whites, one tooth left and that one about to go, eyepatch meant to cover his left eye socket but off the mark and closer to the hole where his left ear once resided. He took a long swig and finished it off, then attempted to smash the empty bottle against the wall, but he lacked the strength and it fell to the floor, rolling back and forth to the gentle harbor sway —

"Argh, why can't the Devil be tardy?" he growled at the

35

figure with the blazing blue eyes that had appeared in the doorless doorway and saluted. "Come to get me? Where's your pitchfork, lavalubber?"

"Captain Hosenpinkel, I am Heinrich von Schatt."

"Argh, the orphaned son of the Devil who collects timetables. The old arsehole doesn't even have the courtesy to come get me himself. Alright, take me down, Zuzanna, I've had enough, argh."

Heinrich remained in the doorway.

"Well, what are ya waitin' for, matey?" Hosenpinkel roared.

"Permission to enter the Wheelhouse, sir."

"What is this nonsense, ya wart scab?"

"I am looking for a ship."

"And what in blazes does the son of Satan want with a ship?"

"I am willing to work as a deckhand, but I plan to someday become a Captain. I already know how to navigate, and I have been charting your ship since my youth. You typically come to port once a month."

"Argh, even an old beardsplitter like me does better than that! But why does Beelzebub II want to be a hand on my dingy?"

"It is my plan to become the greatest Captain who ever lived."

"Argh, 'tis what they all say." Hosenpinkel had declared the same when he was but a lad seeking a ship, and since then had heard a thousand greenhorns utter likewise before boarding the *Maiden* and promptly shitting themselves. Yet, hosed as he was, and soused, the old Captain could see there was something different about this lad. His soul was dark as the sea herself, and, by the way he was stealing glances at the instruments, he must be a born navigator. "You say you can drive this old wench?"

"I can navigate any seafaring vessel."

"Aye, then you'll be of more use to me up here than with those bilge rats down below. Take the helm, First Officer von Schatt, as you're driving this old dumpster from now on. I've always wanted to have a driver. Wahoo! This is the best damn bender I've ever had, argh!"

Just before dusk, Heinrich—who'd never operated a vehicle of any kind, not even a bicycle, but who'd memorized instruction books, manuals, engineer drawings, footnotes, tables of content, and indexes, and had been seeded with navigational gifts that cannot be taught—perfectly guided the *Maiden* out of the Port of Bremerhaven and up the North Sea. Hosenpinkel cheerfully barked orders at his new protégé from the back of the Wheelhouse floor, swigging a fresh bottle of *Whesskey* and swearing off sobriety forever. Through the night they steamed towards Kristiansand, Norway, then, in the days and weeks that followed, the ports of Oslo, Gothenburg, Copenhagen, and the Free City of Danzig, where, after a few days at port, they would turn her around and run the route in reverse.

Up in the Wheelhouse, the lad was a natural and Hosenpinkel didn't have to teach him a thing. Off the boat, though, he knew nothing of the wonders of port, and the old Captain was happy to serve as his mentor.

Though Heinrich refused drink at sea—which some dormant part of Hosenpinkel's conscience knew was a good thing—he was a willing student at port, and there was no better classroom than the Free City, the last outbound stop on the *Maiden*'s route, and home of Hosenpinkel's favorite sailor-friendly house of ill-repute, Slony's Burlesque Theatre. The glow of the red neon BURLESQUE sign buzzing sharply in the window could be seen from a mile out at sea, a beacon that proved too powerful for most jack tars to resist, save those headed to the place up the street where the ladies did not tread. At the front of the joint was a bar where sailors could get a drink, or twelve, before proceeding to the basement theater, where shows started every ten minutes, then they would head to the parlour to pick a girl to take upstairs.

After a shot of *Whesskey* at the bar—which the kid handled well, Hosenpinkel observed, another sign that he was a natural—Captain led First Officer down a staircase to the "theater", which consisted of three rows of splintered church pews facing a two-foot platform stage, in the center of which was a brass fireman's pole bolted to the stage floor and ceiling.

"There is no hole in the ceiling for the fireman's pole," Heinrich observed. "How do the firemen get through?"

"It's not for the firemen, ya swab head! It's for the burlesque dancers!"

"Then how do the burlesque dancers get through?"

"Argh! Wait and see, bung hole!"

It was crowded and they had to sit in the third row. Just before showtime, a hush came over the room, as the beer girl, the shot girl, and the tobacco girl settled their last transactions. The tobacco girl then bent over the Victrola, prompting a round of catcalls and whistles, and dropped the needle on the spinning black circle. After a few seconds of painfully loud scratching, the carousing horns blasted into the room and, from behind the stage curtain, emerged a woman with scandalously short black hair, her hourglass figure clad in shiny black bustier, fishnet stockings, high-heels, and a red feather boa, who grabbed the pole, leaned backwards, and started swinging with a gam high in the air, prompting some of the sailors to start feeling seasick—

"Argh, I'm too squiffy for this," Hosenpinkel said. "I prefer the rooms to spin, not the ladies. Let's get to the parlour and crack Jenny's tea cup, aye."

After the parlour door closed behind them, Captain and First Officer were transported from boisterous burlesque to the soothing flow of Bach's *Jesu, Joy of Man's Desiring*. The octagon-shaped room was covered with plush burgundy carpet, vertically-striped burgundy & buttermilk wallpaper, and velvet burgundy chaise lounges against the wall, only three of which were occupied by availables, all of whom were clad in the same bustiers, fishnet stockings, and high-heels as the dancer.

Upon seeing Hosenpinkel, both Celestyna and Druzella rolled their eyes. For young Wiktoria, though, it was the presence of the younger man that chilled her soul, as if the Devil himself had walked into the room—

"What now?" Heinrich asked his Captain.

"Pick one, then take her upstairs to a room."

"Then what?"

"Argh, blunderbuss, I didn't know you was *this* green! Tell her you want to give her a physical inspection. She'll know what to do, aye."

Celestyna, 27, had arrived at middle-age, but her generous proportions still showed well in the dim parlour lamplight, as did her curly brown hair, rosy-cheeks, and big hands. She was still the most popular in the house among those who preferred a larger lady, which was most sailors.

Druzella, rumored to be over 200 years old, was a pale, skeletal transplant from Transylvania with waist-length black hair, popular with those inclined towards necrophilia, also common among sailors.

Wiktoria, the new girl with the strawberry-blonde curls, was young and pretty like a schoolgirl, without the hardened look the others had, having not yet fully shed the fear in her eye she arrived here with—

"There ya go, squid-nuts, an early hedge-creeper for an unlicked cub," Hosenpinkel said. "I know some addle pates like mophandles with tight crinkums, but tonight I've a hankerin' for some tallow on the tuna, argh."

Resigned to her fate, Celestyna slid off her chaise.

"Good evening, Gerhard," she said.

"Aye, me strumpet."

After Hosenpinkel had gone, Heinrich considered his decision. While there was something appealing about the older, bony one, it was the fear in the green eyes of the younger one that spoke to him—

"You there, young one," Heinrich said. "Take me to your upstairs room for a physical inspection."

Wiktoria slid off the chaise and led him out of the parlour to a caged cashier's window at the foot of the staircase, where Heinrich was charged 20 *zloty* by a heavy bald man with a cigar clenched between his teeth. She then led him up to the third floor, where, behind the closed doors, could be heard all manners of moans, grunts, screams, slaps, and cries. He followed her to the end of the hall, into the only room with an open door.

The room smelled of sauerkraut and was lit by a dim bulb hanging by a cord from the ceiling. There was trash all over the floor, and the only furniture was a stained mattress atop a metal bedframe. A frayed roller shade covered the window.

"My name is Wiktoria," she said, looking down. "What is your name?"

"Heinrich von Schatt, First Officer of the *Iron Maiden*."

"And what is it you would like to do, First Officer Heinrich?"

"On this ship, you are to address me as 'Captain'."

"Oh, I apologize, Captain Heinrich. What is it you would like to do?"

"I would like to give you a physical inspection. However, I do not know how to do this and will need proper instruction."

"First, you must remove your trousers."

"Do I need to remove my shirt?"

"You can, but it is not necessary."

Removing his trousers, Heinrich became distracted watching Wiktoria unhook her bustier and lift it above her navel, revealing a lush bush that excited him further, while she became distracted by the enormity of his uncircumcised thing—

"What do I do now?" Heinrich asked.

"I will bend over, and you will put it in the hole," she said, preferring to do it this way so that the men could not look into her eyes, and so she would not have to look at them. After she had positioned herself with one hand leaning on the mattress to balance herself, she reached back through her legs and spread herself open with her fingers—

"In there," she said.

In her limited experience, most sailors had small ones, and most of them didn't function properly. Thus, she had never encountered one as big and hard as this, and she nearly cried when it was all the way in—

"Something is happening," Heinrich said.

"Already?"

"Yes, a vonderful sensation—"

She felt his climax, then heard something land on the floorboards. She waited a moment before asking if he was finished.

"I believe so," he said. "Now what do I do?"

"It is done. Pull it out and get dressed."

After Heinrich was dressed and Wiktoria re-hooked, she led him out of the room and back down the hall. Halfway to the staircase, Heinrich stopped when he heard Hosenpinkel behind one of the doors yelling, "Take that, wench!" Anxious to inform his mentor of his success, Heinrich, without knocking, opened the door, then froze at the sight of Celestyna bent over the bed, and, behind her, nude Hosenpinkel about to spank her, his own tiny thing buried so deep in his short-and-curlies that he looked like a lady down there—

"Aye, von Schatt, watch and learn!" he said. "This is how ya keep a wagtail in line, argh!" He then proceeded to spank her with the strength of a nancy robin, then looked back at his protégé and roared, "Now get goin', ya duke of limbs, while I finish makin' me mess, argh!"

⚓　⚓　⚓

During those early years, Heinrich didn't think Hosenpinkel was long for the world, a few winters at most, and then he would take over as Captain of the *Maiden*. But the old drunkard proved more resilient than he appeared, seemingly not aging at all, the *Whesskey* preserving his vitality, sobriety a guillotine. Still ahead of where he thought he would be at this point—he'd factored in several years of paying dues as a deckhand, and had never considered that he'd go straight to the Wheelhouse—he remained focused on perfecting his navigational skills in the chilly waters of the North Sea, knowing his time would come.

As late as the autumn of 1935, few in the fleet were paying attention to the political happenings on land, which seemed far off in greater *Deutschland* and had yet to find footing in quiet Bremerhaven. This would change in 1936, when the Nazis finally noticed the quaint little harbor and realized its strategic significance. Suddenly, Third Reich soldiers were everywhere, harassing citizens, shaking down Captains, not hesitating to use their Lugers on anyone who objected.

Down at the end of the pier, the *Iron Maiden* was spared from harassment, the soldiers assuming that such a dilapidated vessel would not be transporting anything of value—especially with her drunkard old captain, who could hardly walk, much less navigate. Their disregard of the *Maiden* caught the attention of Sonny Leberwurst, head of the local rackets, whose family had made a killing smuggling beer and *Whesskey* into the States during Prohibition. He knew what the Nazis didn't, that the *Maiden*, while not pretty, was a seaworthy vessel, and it was captained not by the old drunkard, but by the boy who collected timetables, whose navigational skills were unparalleled in these parts. It was important to the Leberwursts to keep their goods moving out of the country as quickly as possible, so they used their regular ships as decoys and allowed the Nazis to confiscate dummy cargo, while quietly hiring the *Maiden* to transport their most valuable goods overseas.

The von Schatt kid was perfect for the job. He was always on time, and he never said anything to anybody. To show their appreciation, the Leberwursts kept the *Maiden* pantry stocked with *Whesskey*, Pall Malls, and Smith Brothers black licorice throat drops, and gave Captain and First Officer keys to a half-dozen hideout flats all over Bremerhaven. Each month, Heinrich also received a weathered envelope, the contents of which quickly accumulated into a small fortune that, per Hosenpinkel's suggestion, he deposited in banks at every port city on the *Maiden*'s route.

By Christmas Eve, 1936, Hosenpinkel was still going strong, while Heinrich, now 22, was itching for his own command, and was now convinced that the old drunkard was never going to die. But he also knew that these were dangerous times for Captains, and that, if he ascended now, the Nazis would notice and begin harassing him, so it was better to lay low until all this blew over.

Late that afternoon, under a blood orange sky, the *Maiden* cruised into Bremerhaven, where residents now lived in fear of incidental eye contact with the wrong person, or of misspeaking to an unfriendly ear. Hosenpinkel, who, for show, was at the helm as they docked, promptly fell unconscious to the floor as soon as they tied up. Heinrich, knowing the old buzzard would be unconscious for hours, broke routine and lingered in the Wheelhouse, sipping from a fresh bottle of *Whesskey*, enjoying the melancholy of the silent night, recalling the Christmas Eve he first laid eyes on the gleaming *encyclopædia*s in the orphanage common room —

Several hours later, bottle spent, Heinrich disembarked and headed towards tonight's flat up the *Barkhausenstraße*, where not a creature was stirring, the only sound his cobblestone footsteps echoing off the buildings he passed, one of them the orphanage. He stopped outside his old bedroom window and again started thinking about the *encyclopædia*s when, down the street, he heard a man shout, "I am not a Jew!"

A block away, under a dim streetlamp, a Nazi soldier yelled at the man to shut up, then shoved him into an alley between a pair of identical three-story apartment buildings —

Heinrich ran to the alley, where the soldier was pointing his Luger at the old man's forehead —

"Soldier, halt!" Heinrich ordered.

The soldier, thinking it was a superior, turned and was about to salute, but froze when he saw the blazing blue eyes —

"*Sohn des Teufels!*" he cried, the Luger falling from his trembling hand and clacking on the cobblestones —

Heinrich punched the soldier in the jaw, stunning him. Then, from behind, he put him in a headlock, lifting him off his feet and squeezing increasingly tighter. Knowing he would kill the man if he didn't stop, he kept squeezing anyway, until his windpipe crunched like a crab shell in the crook of his arm.

Finally, he let go. The soldier crumpled to the ground, squirming on the cobblestones for air. Then he became still, mouth still agape.

The old man cleared his throat.

"Have you been harmed, sir?" Heinrich asked.

"I believe I am fine," the old man answered. "A little shaken, but fine. And thank you. These Nazi swine are getting worse every day. But what about you, young man? Are you hurt?"

"I am unharmed," Heinrich said.

"This is good. I will not ask your name, and please do not ask mine, as we are, at the moment, in quite the serious pickle, and are better off remaining strangers."

"How do you mean?"

The old man looked at Heinrich in disbelief.

"Do you not realize what you have just done?"

"I saw this soldier attack you. I was merely acting in your defense."

"Oy vey," the old man said, rolling his eyes. "They will not look kindly at one of their own being killed in defense of an old Jew. They will torture and kill us."

"I heard you say you were not a Jew."

"A man will say most anything when his life is in peril. Regardless, what is done is done, and we must hide the body and get away from here. It is only a matter of time before someone notices he is missing."

The alley led from the street to a small courtyard, where, in the corner, there were several stacks of wooden cartons overflowing with trash.

"There," he said to Heinrich, pointing. "Bury the body beneath the trash. Fortunately, it is the Christian holiday, so it will be sitting there for several more days before being brought to the incinerator, and by then you can be long gone from here."

"Won't someone smell the rotting body?"

"It is winter, so it probably won't smell too bad. And they will keep stacking more smelly trash on top of it, so it probably won't be that noticeable, if at all. Regardless, we do not have time to sit around trying to think of a better idea."

Heinrich lifted the lifeless body over his shoulder and carried it to the courtyard. He started moving the trash cartons and cleared a space at the base of the wall, then dragged the body into the space and re-stacked the cartons on top of it. In minutes, the corner looked as it had before, just a pile of trash.

"They are going to be looking all over for him," the old man said, "and, when they find him with a crushed windpipe, they are going to tear this city apart trying to figure out who did it. Which is why you must leave this place forever. Tonight."

"What about you?"

"No one will ever believe that an old man like me had anything to do with crushing a young man's windpipe. But you are big and strong enough to easily do such a thing, as I have now seen with my own eyes, and, if anyone has seen you walking around the area tonight—which is likely, considering that you are a very noticeable man, and that there are many eyes around here watching through the cracks—they will eventually track you down and kill you. Maybe go to Sweden, or even America. But do not stay here. This is no longer *Deutschland*, it is a den of monsters!"

⚓ ⚓ ⚓

Captain Gerhard Hosenpinkel regained consciousness at daybreak, Christmas morning, on the Wheelhouse floor, tongue stuck to the roof of his dry mouth, breathing *Whesskey* and vomit fumes. Despite decades of finding himself in the exact same spot for the exact same reason, it usually took him several minutes to determine where he was and how he'd gotten there.

Today, though, the old coxswain realized immediately that something was amiss. The engines were blasting and von Schatt was at the helm, neither of which were unusual, but he could not hear the noises of the men working below, and it felt too soon for the Christmas break to be over—

"Argh, how long have I been out?" he grumbled, pushing himself up to a sitting position. "Is the Jesus-fest over already?"

"We are on a special trip, sir," Heinrich said. "I attempted to receive your permission to take the vessel beforehand, but I was unable to awaken you to inform you that I have become involved in an emergency situation and have had to leave

Deutschland immediately."

"Leave *Deutschland immediately*, aye," Hosenpinkel repeated, a smile forming at the prospect of a juicy tale of whorehouse hijinks, or an angry father or husband and a mob of townsfolk chasing after the lad. "What have you done, me boy? Did one of yer squishies slip through the nets?"

"I have killed a Nazi soldier, sir."

"A soldier? D'yer mak'er daughter? Wife? Sister? Pony?"

"The soldier was harassing an elderly Jewish man on the *Barkhausenstraße*. The soldier attempted to point his Luger at me, but I intervened and proceeded to crush his windpipe."

Hosenpinkel waited a moment for the rest of the story before finally asking, "Well, d'yer mak'er or not?"

"I do not know to whom you are referring."

"The daughter? The wife? Tell me more, tell me more, did ya get in 'er box?"

"No."

"Aye, there's something satisfying about snatch you don't have to pay for. Of course, I haven't known that satisfaction in forty years—"

"There was no girl."

"Argh, this yarn is getting dull." Hosenpinkel grabbed the *Whesskey* bottle that had been rolling on the floor beside him all night and found a few drops left—

"We are headed to *Göteborg*," Heinrich said. "You will have to navigate the *Maiden* back to Bremerhaven yourself."

"Argh! I haven't navigated this old wench in nearly a decade!"

"I have no choice, sir. I must not return to *Deutschland*."

"So, you're leaving forever?"

"Yes, sir."

"Argh," the old Captain grumbled, softly this time. "I

suppose I knew this day would come. You are too fine a seaman to be humping this old whore the rest of your life, as fine a dumpster she is, aye."

"The *Iron Maiden* will always be special to me for being my first ship."

"An old cherry-popper, she is, aye. But what will you do in *Sverige*? I mean besides rummaging with the blondie pies?"

"I will find a new ship and become a Captain. It will likely not be in *Göteborg*, though, and I ask that you tell no one of my whereabouts."

"I'll say nothing to the swine, aye. But there will be a record of the *Maiden* at *Göteborg*—"

"No. I will disembark prior to *Göteborg*."

"What do ya mean *prior* to *Göteborg*?"

"There is an old beer barrel down in the hold that I will navigate to the shore, just ahead of the pier."

"You will navigate a beer barrel?"

"Yes, sir."

"And who's down there feeding the furnace?"

"No one. I have been running down feeding her myself every hour, and I'll do it once more before I disembark."

"We've no crew?"

"No, sir."

"Argh!"

After nearly a decade of navigating into the Gothenburg Freight Port on the *Göta älv*, Heinrich had intimate knowledge of every current and tidal pattern, and knew precisely where his Captain would have to push the barrel overboard with him in it—off the starboard side as the *Maiden* would be making her U-turn after clearing the Hunnebådan shoal, which would, in conjunction with the wake of the U-turn, carry him along the inbound shipping lane towards, but just short of, the freight port, landing him at a backyard sailboat dock in Majorna, where he would pop off the lid, abandon the barrel, and walk into town as if on an evening stroll.

Before the lid was sealed, Heinrich, standing in the barrel, saluted his Captain one last time.

"Aye," Hosenpinkel said, saluting back. "It's been a pleasure sailin' with ya, lad!"

Heinrich crouched and covered himself with the lid, which Hosenpinkel sealed closed with a mallet. Then, with what little strength the frail Captain had left, he pushed the barrel over the side and watched it drop fifteen feet into the moonlit water, then scuttled up to the Wheelhouse to commence the 36-hour steam back to Bremerhaven, during which he would have to run down and shovel coal into the furnace every hour, while also keeping himself fueled with *Whesskey*—

At this late hour, with most ships still on holiday, the *Maiden* did not encounter another vessel as she steamed around the northern tip of Denmark, then back down the North Sea. Approaching Bremerhaven, though, a bright light in the harbor suddenly appeared against the daybreak sky and began blinking signals at him.

"Argh, what madness is this?" he growled, then took a long swig. There was just enough daylight to see through the spyglass the picket boat with the swastikas painted on her sides, one of the vessels the Nazis used to patrol the harbor. Normally they would be shaking down someone else, but, with the rest of the boats tied to the pier, the *Maiden* was the only vessel on the water.

Hosenpinkel throttled down to DEAD SLOW and signaled back with his light to make them think he was complying. After a long last swig from the bottle, he poured the remaining contents onto the floor –

"Enjoy, my love," he said to his old lady, then opened his *Whesskey* cabinet and began pouring the contents of the remaining bottles on the floor while doing a whooping dance in the pond that was forming. He then retrieved a package of Pall Malls from his uniform coat and lit one with a match from a Slony's matchbook, then set the matchbook aflame and let it fall. The Wheelhouse was soon ablaze, including her Captain, who throttled her to FULL and roared, "This is for you, von Schatt! Argh!"

Expecting compliance, the Nazis had cut their engine, and, at the moment, no one was at the helm. Two of the six on board were stationed at turrets pointed at the *Maiden*, while the other four had lined up port side, Lugers drawn. When one of the turret operators finally realized what was happening and started firing, the rest followed suit. It occurred to none of them, at first, to man the helm and move their 55-footer out of the way, as if their bullets were sufficient to stop the 200-foot rustbucket about to broadside them—

Up in the Wheelhouse, Hosenpinkel roared with laughter, until a bullet pierced the window and passed through his *Whesskey*-rotted skull. He fell backwards, his upended feet catching the helm knobs, keeping the *Maiden* on a steady course forward—

On the picket boat, one of the soldiers finally attempted to take the helm, but it was too late. The *Maiden* sliced the smaller craft in half, but, in doing so, the twisted metal wreckage of the smaller boat cut a ten-foot gash in her starboard hull, and she started taking on water—

The turret operators and the soldier who attempted to man the helm were crushed in the picket boat wreckage, their bodies pierced with metal shards and squirting blood like fountains. The remaining three soldiers on the starboard side had leapt into the water just before impact, but not soon enough to escape the powerful swell that the colliding boats had prompted, pulling them back towards the *Maiden* and slamming their heads against her hull, splitting their skulls open, their lifeless bodies bobbing in the ripples as the two sections of gurgling picket boat sank beside them.

Up in the *Maiden* Wheelhouse, the body of Captain Gerhard Wilhelm Hosenpinkel quietly burned as his old lady lay him down, until she too disappeared beneath the surface, settling into her shallow grave of North Sea muck.

NYNÄSHAMN

1936–1943

In Gothenburg, home of the Volvo factory, Heinrich, after withdrawing his funds at Olaf Savings & Loan—where he had the largest amount, enough that he didn't have to retrieve any more from the other cities on the *Maiden* route—spent several hours walking along the canals and over the footbridges before finally landing in Haga, the old town, where he went into a secondhand book shop and purchased a German-Swedish pocket dictionary—he knew enough *Svenska* to get by in the burlesque houses, but he would have to master the language if he was going to stay in the country. At the café next door, he supped on tiny meatballs with mashed potato and lingonberries, and, for dessert, cinnamon buns and crepes with blueberry jam and exotic butter, and a pineapple ice cream soda.

As much as he admired *Göteborg*, Heinrich knew he could not stay. There were people in this city who knew his face, but, more concerning, she was a common stop for Bremerhaven boats—if any of the *Deutsch* Captains or crews spotted him here, it would quickly be known to all back home where he was. A safer place would be Stockholm, where Bremerhaven boats seldom ventured, and most of the shipping routes were northeasterly to Finland and Russia.

After his meal, he walked to the *Centralstation*, where he

found the Office of the Travel Bureau. He browsed the rack of brochures and pamphlets, many for boat tours and rafting adventures, until one caught his eye, a trifold for the Port of Nynäshamn, with a photograph on the cover of a gleaming modern ferry-ship named the *Var Så God*, and a slogan beneath:

Nynäshamn: Spännande och Nytt!

He consulted his dictionary—

"Nynäshamn: Exciting and New!" he said, tapping on the pamphlet, thinking that no one would ever find him in a place that even he'd never heard of.

In all the years he'd been coming to *Göteborg* on the *Maiden*, he'd never taken occasion to visit the *Centralstation*, which he discovered to be an architectural marvel of steel and glass. It was early afternoon, clouds of tobacco smoke hovering motionless near the ceiling windows, through which the golden beams of the northern winter sun showcased the display stand below stocked with freshly printed timetables for all the different rail lines. Heinrich stopped to collect one of each, pleasantly lightheaded from the complement of tobacco and ink fumes, then stood in queue for the ticket window, purchasing a one-way to Stockholm.

He had no memory of ever being on a train, yet the experience seemed familiar. He'd been expecting to see giant black locomotives like the ones in his old *Encyclopædia*s spewing sooty smoke from chimneys, with cowcatchers in the front and a little red caboose bringing up the rear, but these were modern, high-speed vessels powered by electricity supplied through wires above the tracks, capable of making the 250-mile trip to Stockholm in under four hours. There were no direct lines from Gothenburg to Nynäshamn on the SJ—*Statens Järnvägar*, the Swedish State Railway—so he would have to take the *Västra Stambanan*, the Western Main Line, to Stockholm, then change to a local commuter train that would make thirteen stops on its way south and take a little over an hour to get there.

Standing on the train pier—which he would soon learn was referred to as a "platform"—he consulted his dictionary and asked a fellow waiting passenger where the front of the vessel would stop so he could get a seat close to the wheelhouse and watch the train Captain navigate. He was directed to the east end of the station, where he waited with great anticipation, but was ultimately disappointed at only being able to catch a brief glimpse of the Captain in the window, whom he saluted as the front of the locomotive passed by. After boarding, he was again disappointed to discover that the locomotive was off-limits, and that the wheelhouse could not be seen from the first passenger car.

Otherwise, the train was a wonder. He was fascinated by how smooth and quiet it was, and how the route was determined by switches that enabled navigation from one track to another. Accustomed to seeing only coastlines, he was taken by the flat countryside, the large winter-brown fields, the horses, the cows, and the dark blue lakes, the latter prompting a deep contemplation on inland waterways that gave him a headache.

In the village of Alingsås, there was a very curious-looking man standing at the crossing waiting for the train to pass, who had wild, unkempt white hair and matching beard, wearing a red suit with white trim. Suddenly, Heinrich felt feverish and was overwhelmed with a sense of *déjà vu*, convinced he had seen this man before, also from a train window—

By 3:00 pm, it was too dark to see anything out the window, so he studied his Swedish for a spell, then stared at the *Var Så God* on the cover of the brochure, picturing himself standing over her helm, navigating her through the cold Baltic waters—

Stockholm *Centralstation* was similar to *Göteborg*, but the night hour in an unfamiliar city made it seem less welcoming. He stopped at the timetable stand and collected one of each for all the lines, then went to the ticket window and purchased a one-way, off-peak on the Nynäshamn local, departing at 9:06 on Track 6.

There were only a few people on the platform. He determined where the front of the train would stop, again hoping to see the Captain navigate—a possibility, since the commuter trains were different than the long-distance SJ rolling stock, in which the Captain sat up high in a locomotive wheelhouse, whereas, in these, the Captain sat in a tiny booth within the front passenger car. While these trains also ran on electricity, they were powered not by wires above the tracks, but by a 900-volt conductor rail built into the ground, the "third rail", that ran alongside the wheel rails.

As the train approached, Heinrich snapped to a saluting position, and had a clear view of the Captain in his wheelhouse booth, one hand on the throttle, the other on the brake lever. But this is the only rail navigation he would witness, as, inside the car, the wheelhouse door was closed. He was the only passenger in the car, and he could see nothing of the landscape out the window. He followed the progress of the train on the timetable, impressed by the precision, and watched the doors slide open and closed thirteen times, until the train pulled into Nynäshamn at 10:26

pm, right on schedule.

The village was dark and still, except for some activity inside the *Sex-Tio*—the Six-Ten, a tiny convenience store down on the corner, a block from the pier. In the store window on the first floor, there was a man sweeping and shutting lights, while, in one of the second floor windows, a woman was putting a little girl to bed.

Down at the harbor, the voluptuous silhouette of the *Var Så God* awaited beneath the moonlit winter sky—

"Ahoy, my love," he said as he approached on the pier. "You will be mine in short order. Where is your owner?"

As if she'd whispered it in his ear, he turned and spied a dimly lit sign on the building indicating the entrance to the passenger waiting room, and the office of Nordic Princess Ferry-Ship Lines, which he knew from the brochure.

The place was deserted, but the bulbs were burning in the waiting room, and the door was unlocked. Inside, there were benches, a restroom, and a display stand with timetables for the 300-foot state-of-the-art *Var Så God* that ran weekly trips for passengers and motorcars to Visby on the isle of Gotland; Liepāja and Ventspils, in Latvia; Tallinn, Estonia; Turku and Helsinki, in Finland; and St. Petersburg, Russia. The next scheduled departure was the day after tomorrow, which explained why, at the moment, no one was here.

He pivoted down the corridor leading to the Nordic Princess office, where the out-of-office cuckoo clock sign on the door indicated they would return at 8:00.

After visiting the head, he went back to the waiting room and stretched himself out on one of the benches, falling asleep to the comforting thought that he was spending his first night at his new home port, convinced that no one from his old life would ever find him here—

⚓ ⚓ ⚓

Jörgen Jonsson, owner and president of Nordic Princess Ferry-Ship Lines, a short, overweight, mustachioed man often mistaken for American moving picture star Oliver Hardy, winced after stepping out of the *Sex-Tio* with his buttered *Wasabröd* and coffee, his ulcers flaring up again two days after losing his third Captain this year. If he did not find a new Captain today, the *Var Så God* would not depart on schedule the next morning, and sorely needed fares would not be collected — which, in all likelihood, would spell the end of Nordic Princess, and, perhaps, Jonsson himself, with a bank payment due in two days, and, right behind that, payments owed to some more worrisome creditors.

As if he didn't have enough on his mind this morning, upon arriving at the office, he found a large young man waiting outside the door, whom he assumed was there to collect on some already-forgotten cockfighting bet he'd been on the short end of —

"What do you want?" Jonsson barked.

"I am Captain Heinrich von Schatt," he said in Swedish. "I am interested in the *Var Så God*."

"*You* are a Captain?"

"Yes."

"By your accent, you sound like a *Deutsch*."

"This is accurate. I had to leave *Deutschland* because of the political situation."

"Yes, yes, the political situation. Do you have a Captain's license?"

"No, sir. However, I can navigate seafaring vessels of any size. If I had been navigating the *RMS Titanic*, she would still be steaming today."

Jonsson was taken by the young man's confidence and invited him into his office.

"You may be my savior, Captain von Schatt," he said, leaning back in his chair, causing it to squeak loudly. "Two days ago we lost our Captain—God rest his soul—to a severe case of Russian dysentery—a truly horrific way to go, I can assure you—and I have spent the last 48 hours turning over every stone looking for a Captain, but all I can find are cheese squat and herring waste, if you know what I mean. I have even wired other ports in the region, but the Captains do not want to come here. There is not enough here, they say. We have no burlesque house or other entertainments in our quiet little village, except for the moving picture house. They want to be where the action is—Stockholm, *Göteborg*, Malmö. Would such a quiet place as ours be fine for you?"

"I have been to the noisy ports. I now seek a quiet port."

"I believe I understand, Captain von Schatt," Jonsson said, grinning. "Despite our ongoing marketing efforts, the true appeal of our little village is that it is quiet, and, if there is someone looking for you, they would never find you here. This is often why past Captains have come here, to get a little peace and quiet, yes. And, if you really can navigate, the paperwork would not be a problem. I know people who can set you up with a *Sverige* passport and Captain's license. However, you must be absolutely truthful—are you really capable of navigating a vessel of this size?"

"Yes," Heinrich said, blue eyes ablaze.

"Very well," Jonsson said, picking up the receiver from the telephone on his desk and ordering someone to fire up the *Var Så God*.

The Bridge was nothing like the *Maiden* Wheelhouse, loaded with the latest navigational equipment and Captain's amenities, sans drunk old coxswain passed out in a puddle of vomit. Heinrich inspected the instruments, strumming her brass with his fingers, whispering the things he would do to her, which made Jonsson a little nervous that this guy might be some nutjob ferryspotter who'd conned him into gaining access to the Bridge—

"I am ready," Heinrich finally announced.

"Therefore, I will ask once more," Jonsson said, leaning in, "because this ship is very big and very expensive, and if anything should happen to her, I would be ruined—but only after I first made sure you are ruined even worse, if you know what I mean—can you really navigate this vessel?"

"Yes," Heinrich said, blue eyes blazing, trousers hitched.

The young Captain's confidence once more cast a spell over Jonsson, who stood aside and watched him approach her helm and wrap his left hand around one of her knobs, then slide his right hand onto her throttle. His concerns began to subside seeing how his lady responded to being touched in such a way, and he was truly impressed when von Schatt navigated the tight channel from pier to open harbor in a single turn, which no previous Captain of this large ferry-ship had ever been able to do in this small port—the others had to stop and back her into position in order to clear the buoy marking the edge of the rocky shallows. So smooth was his command, with precision unseen in these waters since the 1912 Olympic sailing regatta—*Sverige* taking the gold in the ten metre with *Kitty*, helmed by Filip "Fillie-Chops" Ericsson— Heinrich followed Jonsson's direction up the harbor, making a perfect starboard turn at the tip of Norra Stegholmen, then gracefully arcing into a port side U-turn around the tiny rock island lighthouse on Finnhällen, and back down the harbor towards the terminal, through the narrow channel, gently into her slip—

"Perfect!" Jonsson exclaimed, saluting, then hugging, his new Captain. "I will take care of your paperwork, and also pick up some Captain's Whites that will actually fit you—my last several Captains were short, and a little messy. Can you navigate tomorrow?"

"I can navigate any day," Heinrich said.

"Excellent. Have you a place to stay in town?"

"I do not."

"This is not a problem. I happen to know of a vacancy, a room above the convenience store up the street. A nice little family resides there. You can see the *Var Så God* right out the window. How does this sound?"

"This sounds satisfactory," Heinrich said, then saluted his new boss.

⚓   ⚓   ⚓

At the age of six, Ingrid's parents, Fjölner and Svea Sandström—*Far* and *Mor*—allowed her to sit behind the *Sex-Tio*'s cash register, with the idea that this would improve her mathematics skills. She was not a dumb child, but she was prone to prolonged daydreaming spells at the schoolhouse, where she was in her second year and had thus far received poor grades, and was perpetually a step or two behind the other children. She did, though, enjoy sitting behind the huge cash register that weighed more than she did, interacting with and making change for the customers, and, as her little fingers became adept at punching the keys, her mathematics skills did improve. At first the customers were humored by exchanging money with a six-year-old girl kneeling on a stool behind the counter, but she usually got the transactions right, and they learned to appreciate her because she knew where everything was, including their "Saturday sweet" candies, the *Sockerbit Chewy Delights* in *Elefantskumfotter* and *Rambo Twist*, and she also knew how to work the *Slörpee* machine—*Far*'s frozen concoction of crushed ice, lingonberry syrup, and Absolut vodka. In the evenings, she would help *Mor* prepare dinner upstairs, which she enjoyed, preferring domestic tasks over school and homework, but, in both places, she was prone to spells where she would be unresponsive.

"Do you think there is something wrong with the child?" Svea asked her husband one evening.

"It is perfectly normal for a girl not to perform well at the schoolhouse," Fjölner said.

"Do you think we should talk to the doctor?"

"And ask him what? Do you have medicine to help with spelling lessons?"

"Oh, Fjölner, you're impossible!"

Just after Christmas, 1936, another of their tenant Captains died. The next day, Mr. Jonsson showed up with Captain von Schatt, and *Mor* took her upstairs *"to allow the men to discuss affairs of business"*, which was the arrangement of renting the newly vacant room to the handsome young Captain—quite the departure from the filthy old men who usually rented the space and died within six months. Just outside the room, there was a separate staircase entrance so that the tenant would not have to pass through their side of the apartment, but everyone had to share the lone bathroom. When the Captain was home, he would leave his shaving supplies on the sink, and she would run her fingers on his razor and pick it up to smell the lingering aroma. In her room, she would drift away, running across prairies, bare feet trampling flowers, sun in her eyes, to her secret grove of Ornäs birch, where she would spend the afternoon unseen by the outside world, never wanting to leave —

Unlike the others, Captain von Schatt did not die. He bought Pall Mall cigarettes, Smith Brothers black licorice throat drops, and *Höhler Whesskey*, the latter becoming more difficult to procure because it came from *Deutschland*, but *Far* knew a guy and sold it to von Schatt with a 400% markup, which, surprisingly, he never complained about. Despite his obvious importance to the family income, Ingrid could tell that her parents did not like the man, which made him even more intriguing —

"He is very dark," she once heard *Mor* say to *Far*, both unaware she was listening at the top of the stairs. "It is like he has no soul."

"I know what you mean, my love," *Far* said. "But he has paid a very generous sum up front for his rent, and we make a very high markup on his goods. A *very* high markup. I cannot turn down such a lucrative arrangement, even if it was with the Devil himself, much less a *Deutsch*."

The only thing Ingrid liked about going to the schoolhouse was seeing Uwe Carlsson, the shy, skinny boy with hair the color of the Scandinavian summer sun, and eyes as blue as the northern morning sky. He was a peculiar boy, though, earnest in his goal of becoming a dentist, planning on spending the rest of his life in Nynäshamn, and even knowing which house he was going to live in when he grew up. After Captain von Schatt moved in, though, she began to realize she would never be as happy here with Uwe as she would be traveling the world with a strong, handsome man who'd been to the other side of the sea.

Ingrid had been nowhere else save Stockholm, where the family would make their annual holiday pilgrimage on the day before Christmas Eve. *Far* would close the store early and they would get on the train, and it would be dark in the middle of the afternoon, and very cold, but the big city would be lit with unbridled Christian joy, and they would walk around Gamla Stan visiting the shops and stop somewhere for hot cocoa. The other big excitement each year happened at the end of the summer, the Nynäshamn Harbor Festival, which, stirring as it was to see the town in full bloom—festival flags waving in the Baltic breeze, Scandinavian-themed placards strung from downtown streetlamps, colorful sailboats gliding around the old Viking ships in the harbor, vendors on the pier selling knick-knacks and tasty treats of parsley, sage, bitters, and gummy fish—she was never able to enjoy, because, as soon as she allowed herself to, it would go too fast and suddenly be over, and she would sink into a deep depression watching them pack up and turn the village back to its dreary self. There would be nothing left to look forward to until Christmas, except for the occasional visit from *Mor*'s cigar-chomping great-uncle, Torkel Nyström, a short, stout 53-year-old bald man who looked more like 73 and worked at the Stockholm Post Office, where he had lost the middle and ring fingers of his right hand in the sorting machine. Most of his teeth were also gone, and the few still left were tarred brownish-yellow. His breath reeked of whiskey, tobacco, and opium, the latter a habit inspired by his hero, Sherlock Holmes, adventures of whom he pilfered from used bookshops and carried with him in the pocket of his tattered black overcoat.

Ingrid did not see his flaws, only his goodness. He always had a gift for her, and had once brought a hand-carved wooden Dala horse painted red with a harness of white, green, blue, and gold, and flowers in its mane. He claimed it had been given him by "a man who lives in the forest", which Fjölner knew was a lie, having seen the very same toy at every gift shop in Gamla Stan, figuring the old fool lifted it from one of them and was probably the real reason he was short a couple of fingers. He would even steal from the *Sex-Tio* right after they had just given him whatever he'd asked for, a habit Svea believed was not intentional, but due to a malady that compelled him to do such things without realizing it.

"Somewhere out on that horizon," he once told her, "out beyond the harbor lights, there's a big, beautiful world out there, and someday you will get to see it."

In the summer of 1940, *Gone with the Wind* came to the moving picture house. For the next three months, every Saturday afternoon, Ingrid, now ten, would spend her allowance to see it. From her first viewing, she recognized Scarlett O'Hara's romantic dilemma as her own, seeing Ashley Wilkes as Uwe Carlsson, and Rhett Butler as Captain von Schatt. With each viewing, she became more annoyed at Scarlett's obsession with Ashley, thinking she should have chosen Rhett, a man who'd traveled the world, who could have saved her and given her a good life. Uwe, like Ashely to Scarlett, had shown no interest, and eventually became an object of her scorn. Whenever she caught herself thinking about him, she became angry at herself for behaving like Scarlett.

Then, in 1943, came *Casablanca*, and there was Ingrid Bergman, the girl from Stockholm, all grown up and making pictures in Hollywood, playing Ilsa Lund, and, again, there was Captain von Schatt, this time Rick Blaine, played by Humphrey Bogart. Through the smoke in the movie house, and the smoke in the film, she saw the dream, and knew of only one man who could make it come true.

After *Casablanca*, she started experimenting with *Mor*'s makeup. She put it on whenever the *Var Så God* was scheduled to arrive or depart, occasions when Captain von Schatt would come into the store. *Mor* rarely ever wore makeup, only when they went to Stockholm, or during the Harbor Festival, or when somebody died, so her supply was limited to a couple of shades of lip paint, a small tin of rouge, and blue eye shadow.

Heinrich, seeing Ingrid for the first time with her adult face on, said, "I see you are no longer a girl-child, but a female lady. You must have many suitors trying to make you a wife."

"Just one," she lied. "His name is Uwe Carlsson, but I do not like him as much as he likes me. He wants to be a dentist."

"Is this not a respectable profession?"

"I suppose. But it is not as exciting as a ship Captain."

"Of course not."

"I like someone else more."

"And who would be this lucky man?"

"It is a secret," she said, blushing, hardly noticeable under the rouge. "What about you? Why do you not have a wife?"

"I am a man of the sea. The *Var Så God* is my wife."

"I meant a real wife. A lady. Do you not get lonesome at night?"

Heinrich had never considered himself lonely, having always had a plethora of women available to him at every port—but her question brought to mind Hosenpinkel, whom he'd never thought of as lonely either. Perhaps he had been lonely, and, without a woman to anchor himself to, his demons were able to have their way, sinking any greater aspirations he may have had. Heinrich recalled his own boyhood aspirations, which had been pushed aside by the success of navigating such an impressive modern vessel as the *Var Så God*, and his keen ear began to pick up a distant moan, which he believed to be coming from the coordinates—

"Perhaps this is true some of the time," he answered. "I am not lonely when I am at sea, but there are times when I am in the room upstairs that I feel alone."

"A ship does not make a good wife. Only a lady makes a good wife."

His blazing blue eyes did not frighten her as it did others, to her they were beacons from the outside world—

"Have you seen *Casablanca*?" she asked.

"I have not yet navigated to that part of the world."

"No, the film, silly," she giggled.

"I am not aware of this film."

"It stars Ingrid Bergman. She is a beautiful actress from Stockholm. Now she is a big star in Hollywood. I want to go to America like her."

"Do you desire to become a film actress?"

"I would settle for going to America. I do not want to stay in this village forever like Uwe Carlsson."

They stopped talking when they heard Fjölner climbing the ladder from the storage cellar. Upon surfacing, he looked first at his daughter's makeup-covered face, then at von Schatt—

"Good evening, Captain," he said. "Is there something with which I can help you?"

"Everything is satisfactory, Mr. Sandström," Heinrich said.

"Are you shipping out this morning?"

"Yes, and I must take leave now. Give my regards to Mrs. Sandström."

"I will do that," Fjölner said, keeping an eye on him until he'd exited the store, then watching him through the window as he headed towards the pier. He then turned to his daughter and growled, "Go wash that hideous mess off your face. And no more cashier. Your mathematics skills are now satisfactory. From now on you will focus strictly on your Bible studies and feminine duties."

The world darkened. Ingrid slid off the stool and climbed the stairs, locking herself in the bathroom, crying as she stood over the sink washing her face, makeup-stained tears dropping into the soapy water—

That evening, on the Bridge of the *Var Så God*, Heinrich could not stop thinking about the girl, now a lady. The rare distraction while navigating unnerved him, and he could only push it aside after deciding he must take action to make it stop.

Five days later in Nynäshamn, he entered the *Sex-Tio* expecting to find Ingrid behind the register, but instead found Mr. Sandström—

"Good evening, Captain von Schatt," Fjölner said.

"Good evening, Mr. Sandström. I am surprised to not see Ingrid here."

"The girl must concentrate on her Bible study and feminine duties."

"Yes, her feminine duties. I am sure she will make a fine wife someday."

Fjölner furrowed his brow. "Under Svea's tutelage, I presume this will someday be the case. But it is no concern of yours, Captain von Schatt."

"Actually, Mr. Sandström, I am relieved to find you here instead of Ingrid, as there is a matter of business I must discuss with you."

Fjölner raised an eyebrow. "I am listening, Captain von Schatt."

"I am here to offer 3,000 *kronor* for your permission to make Ingrid my bride. This is a generous sum for a common girl from a small village, and I will also waive the dowry. All of this, of course, is on the condition that she is still a virgin."

Fjölner, flush with rage, said through gritted teeth, "Captain von Schatt, you must now leave and never return. I will refund the remaining rent paid to Mr. Jonsson, but afterwards I wish to never see you in this store or apartment house again!"

"Would you reconsider if I raised the offer to 4,000?"

"Gather your belongings and get out!" Fjölner roared.

Ingrid listened to the exchange from the top of the stairs. When she heard the jingle of the little bell above the store door, she rushed down the tenant staircase, intercepting Captain von Schatt at the bottom—

"Captain—Heinrich—" she said. "I want to be your bride."

"Your *Far* has not given permission for this."

"He is mean and I do not care what he thinks."

Heinrich looked at the harbor, then back at Ingrid.

"I have heard the Americans are building ships faster than they can find Captains," he said.

"Are you going to America?"

"Yes. To New York."

"Please take me with you. You will be lonely in America without a bride."

"Are you aware that America is a country at war?"

"Yes, but there will always be war."

"If you agree to be my bride, you must always obey my orders."

"Yes, Heinrich."

They looked into each other's eyes. In his, Ingrid saw the gleaming streets of America, where she would be free from *Far*'s tyranny, and be the wife of a handsome, noble Captain. In hers, Heinrich saw the birth of his son, the First Male Heir, who would inherit a maritime legacy to be celebrated for generations.

"Then it is settled. We will wed, and you will accompany me to New York. But you must wait several days while I make the arrangements, and carry on with your daily activity as if you were going to stay in Nynäshamn forever. You must say nothing of this to anyone. If your *Far* learns of this plan, he will lock you in the cellar, and I will leave for America without you. Do you have a passport or traveling paperwork?"

"No. I have not been anywhere beyond Stockholm."

"This should not be a problem, but I will make sure there will be no issues. If you are serious about this adventure, then you must follow my instructions exactly. Go back upstairs as if you had not seen or spoken to me. Pack your belongings and compose a note informing your parents that you are entering a convent in Finland, then meet me Thursday night at 11:30 in the alley behind Löfgren's Fish Store. Leave the note on your pillow for your parents to find in the morning. If you are not there when I arrive at precisely 11:30, I will leave without you. At that time we will leave Nynäshamn, then *Sverige*, permanently. Until then, do everything as you normally would when in front of others. I will be out of town making preparations. But you must go upstairs now before your parents see us speaking, and you must not mention a word of this to anyone. This is an order."

"Yes, Heinrich."

Before going back upstairs, Ingrid stood on her toes and kissed her fiancé on the lips—

No lady had ever kissed him like this. Such affections were discouraged in the burlesque houses, and Heinrich didn't like getting his face daubed with greasy lip paint. But this was different, and he couldn't stop thinking about it on his way to Mr. Jonsson's office —

⚓   ⚓   ⚓

Jörgen Jonsson, behind his desk sorting the trip receipts and cooking the books, tried to stay focused, but was unable to stop thinking about that evening's cockfights, on which he had placed several large wagers. He was then further distracted by a knock on the door, in direct defiance of his standing order to all office personnel that he not, under *any* circumstances, be disturbed when the "DO NOT DISTURB" placard was hung on his doorknob. He waited a moment, thinking the guilty party would realize his mistake and go away, but, after a second knock, he slammed the receipts down and demanded to know who was there.

"It is Captain von Schatt," Heinrich said through the door.

"Oh, yes, one moment, Captain," he responded, suddenly polite, sliding the receipts into his top desk drawer, wondering what this could be about since von Schatt was a stickler to routine and had never once in nearly seven years come to the office after returning from a trip. "Please come in."

After salutes were exchanged and von Schatt was seated, Jonsson asked, "What can I do for you, Captain von Schatt?"

"I have come to resign as Captain of the *Var Så God*, effective immediately."

"Resign?" Jonsson's heart started pounding. "But why?"

"It is a personal reason. I will be leaving *Sverige* to pursue other interests."

"Where will you go?"

"I cannot disclose this. But I am leaving Nynäshamn immediately."

"Is it the money? I can pay you more—"

"It is not a financial matter."

"Can I then convince you to stay a little longer? At least until I find another Captain?"

"This is not possible, Mr. Jonsson. I must depart immediately."

Gambling debts, late payment penalties owed the bank, vigs on top of vigs owed Carlo "The Sicilian" Panini, the ports of Helsinki and St. Petersburg hiking their docking fees, the War wreaking havoc on ridership—he would need a miracle at the cockfights if he were going to survive this time—

There were no miracles that evening. Now owing substantially more money to several additional dangerous people, and no longer having a Captain to navigate his main source of income, Jonsson, despite his generous proportions, managed to slip unseen out the back door of Alborg's chicken shack before the card was finished, and return safely to the Nordic Princess office. He knew they would already be looking for him and be there within minutes, but he took a moment to reflect upon the vacant desks, typewriters, chairs, and the water cooler, before stepping inside his own office and gently closing the door.

Flopping into his squeaky chair, he retrieved from the lower desk drawer "Shorty", his loaded 1929 Russian Nagant revolver, put his mouth around the barrel, and pushed the trigger with his thumb—

⚓ ⚓ ⚓

In the Stockholm dusk, Heinrich walked briskly over Riksbron Bridge, between the Parliament buildings, and onto the cobblestones of Gamla Stan, pivoting through the maze of narrow thoroughfares lined with restaurants, taverns, and souvenir shops, until arriving at *Carlo's Gifts*, its storefront sign featuring the flags of Sweden, Italy, and the three-legged Sicilian coat of arms.

Inside, he found the exiled Carlo "The Sicilian" Panini—third cousin of Don Verrazano Panini of Scoglitti, the most feared man in *la cosa nostra*—dozing off on a stool behind the counter, in front of him a half-empty glass of red wine next to an unlabeled green bottle, and a half-smoked cigar burned out in a ceramic Swedish flag ashtray. There were no customers, and, by the undisturbed dust on the shelves of Dala horses and Viking figurines, it appeared there hadn't been for some time.

"Greetings, Mr. Panini!" Heinrich said, saluting.

Carlo snorted awake. It took a moment to focus on the man who'd provided him safe passage on the *Var Så God* from Torku to Nynäshamn, the last sea leg of his flight from Sicily—

"Captain von Schatt!" he exclaimed, face alit, sliding off the stool, shaking his hand, hugging him, kissing his cheeks—

"Hello, Mr. Panini," Heinrich said, unnerved by the kissing—

"Stop with this 'Mister' business. Call me 'Carlo', as you are a friend, and an honorable man—unlike that employer of yours, who is a scoundrel and a thorn in the foot—though it pains me that you have never come and asked for the favor I am waiting to repay for providing me safe passage after I had to leave my homeland, which, of course, you understand as well as I."

"I have come to ask for the favor."

"Ah, Carlo is happy to hear this! But first let me put the sign up and bolt the door, then we will go in the back and pour some wine and talk."

The back room looked like an authentic Italian restaurant, dimly lit, red-and-white gingham tablecloths, exposed brick, paintings of narrow Sicilian streets, of men pushing fishing boats into the sea, of women picking grapes—

He offered Heinrich a seat at one of the tables while retrieving another glass, which he placed in front of his guest and filled with wine from the green bottle.

"So, what can Carlo do for Captain von Schatt?"

"I am no longer Captain of the *Var Så God*."

"What? No more 'Captain'? What has happened?"

"I have met a young lady."

"Oh, it is *that* kind of favor," Carlo laughed.

"The young lady has agreed to be my bride, yet her father, who is also my landlord, is opposed. I have offered him 3,000 *kronor* for her, and even increased it to 4,000, but he became angry and has evicted me."

"Ah, I see. You need someone to help him change his mind."

"I do not think he will change his mind."

"You would be impressed by how quickly Carlo can change his mind."

"At this point, the father is of no consequence. The girl has agreed to be my bride."

"What is the girl's name?"

"Ingrid."

"Ah, Ingrid. Very pretty name—like the beauty in the moving pictures, only younger, I presume, ah—"

"I am uncertain of her exact age. She wears makeup on her face, yet still attends the schoolhouse with Uwe Carlsson."

"Who is this Uwe Carlsson?"

"Her suitor, an aspiring dentist."

"Is your Ingrid enrolled in the dental schoolhouse?"

"No. It is a regular schoolhouse."

"I see," Carlo said, sipping his wine. "Do you need me to take care of this Uwe Carlsson for you?"

"This will not be necessary. My Ingrid wants to go to America, like the moving picture star Ingrid you have mentioned. I too want to go to America and Captain one of the great new ships they are building for the War effort. It is my understanding that they are desperate for Captains. But I was not anticipating this outcome with her *Far*, nor was it my intention to inconvenience Mr. Jonsson, who does not have a Captain at the moment—"

"Do not worry about Mr. Jonsson. I will personally make sure he is taken care of."

"Thank you, Carlo. I am relieved to hear this. Yet, at the moment, I have no ship or place to stay, and I have instructed Ingrid to leave a note to her parents informing them that she has left home to enter a convent in Finland. She is then to sneak out and meet me behind Löfgren's Fish Store at 11:30 Thursday night, and I have promised to take her to America."

"Ah, very good, Heinrich, classic misdirection. One pair goes one way, and the other pair goes the other way."

"Yes. One will be navigating east, and the other will be navigating west."

"They will look for her in Finland, while you and she will be honeymooning in America."

"Correct. However, this is where the plan ends, and I am unsure how to proceed."

"I see, I see. The picture is now clear. You were wise to come see Carlo, as he is the man who can help you achieve your dreams. It just so happens that one of our ships—*Da Brooklyn Mama*—will be docking at *Göteborg* on Monday night and departing the following evening. She will make one stop at Southampton, England, and from there will steam to Brooklyn, New York. As long as you and your Ingrid can get to *Göteborg* before Tuesday night, it will be smooth sailing. My nephew, Carmine, is also traveling to America on *da Mama* that night. He is a Roman-Catholic priest ordained by the Pope himself, and also a doctor who will be working at The Infant Jesus Hospital on Long Island in New York. The reason this is of interest to you is that he can provide a genuine Vatican-issued marriage certificate, which will be helpful to have once you are in America, and he will also be able to get any other paperwork she will need through my family in New York. I will also help you get to *Göteborg*, as I happen to own a Volvo dealership up near the University. After you leave here, take the train to the University stop, and there will be a man there who will hand you the key and title to a new PV444, all legal. This way you can pick up your Ingrid on Thursday night and drive her straight to *Göteborg*. This is much safer than traveling on the national railway, where you would be seen by many faces. When you arrive in *Göteborg*, you can stay in one of our safehouses until it is time to depart. You will drive the Volvo right onto *Da Brooklyn Mama*—she is a freighter, so we have room in the cargo hold. I have heard it is necessary to have an automobile in America—she is a big country with great distances between cities, and in New York there is a man named Moses trying to convert every square mile into highways to make it easier for the *pezzonovantes* to drive their fancy motorcars to the parks. Just before docking in Brooklyn, you will put Ingrid in the trunk, but you will show the officials your passport, so they will witness that you arrived alone, and it will also be easier for you to find a new ship if you enter the country legally. So, my friend, what do you think of this plan?"

"This all sounds wise. I will pay for the Volvo, of course."

"Nonsense! This is my wedding gift to you, and a token of my appreciation for what you did for me all those years ago. Just be ready to pick up your Ingrid on Thursday night, then drive her directly to the address in *Göteborg* I am about to give you—"

⚓   ⚓   ⚓

At her bedroom window, the first drops of an autumn storm pattering the glass, Ingrid, Dala horse in hand, gazed at the harbor lights, still angry at *Far* for evicting her Captain, and for the cheerfulness he had displayed since, culminating the evening before, when he gave free blueberry *Slörpees* to the three customers in the store at 6:10 pm.

Thursday morning, she followed her normal routine, except, upon her arrival at the schoolhouse, she went out of her way to say hello to Uwe Carlsson at his desk, which she hadn't done in some time. This mattered not to the boy, who mumbled *hej* without looking up from his dental supply catalog, her final reminder that this was a child compared to the man who would take her to America, and that there was nothing here worth waiting for.

After school, she stuck to the routine—homework, helping *Mor* prepare supper, bath, and Bible reading, until *Mor* came in at 10:00 to say good night, kissing her forehead, gently closing the door. In tears, she listened to *Far* downstairs locking the store, then his boots scraping up the steps and the hallway floor creaking towards her room. The door opened and he stuck his head in—

"Good night, my love," he said.

"Good night, *Far*," she said, coldly.

At precisely 11:30 pm, a heavy rain falling, Heinrich, behind the wheel of his new firebrick red 1943 Volvo PV444, turned into the alley between Löfgren's Fish Store and Ida's Beauty Parlor. At the end of the alley, in the harsh light of the headlamps, stood his bride-to-be, drenched, shivering, holding at her side a stuffed laundry sack.

Ignoring the rain, leaving the engine running and the headlamps on, Heinrich stepped out of the car and approached her—

"Good evening, Ingrid."

"Good evening, Heinrich."

"From this moment forward, whenever I arrive or depart, by land or by sea, you will stand at attention saluting. During arrival, you will hold your salute until I have disembarked the vessel and returned the salute. During departure, you will hold the salute until the vessel is no longer in view. Is this understood?"

"But, Heinrich, I do not know how to salute—"

"Like this," he said, demonstrating. "Right hand to forehead, elbow crooked at precisely 45 degrees."

It took a few tries, but she finally did it well enough to receive a return salute. Heinrich then opened the passenger door for her and she crawled inside, while he pivoted around to the driver's side. After backing out of the alley, the Volvo roared out of Nynäshamn and into the Scandinavian night, commencing the 300-mile journey west to *Göteborg*, but first north on the Nynäsvägen to get around Himmerfjärden Bay. At Norrköping, the smell of the Volvo's interior, hardly noticeable at first, started making Ingrid nauseous, a sweet, sickly combination of breadcrumbs, molasses, orange marmalade, damp tobacco, male body odor, onion—

"I am going to be sick!" she cried.

Heinrich pulled over just in time for her to open the door and vomit on the side of the road —

"Your seasickness has caused a delay," he said afterward. "Do not let it happen again."

"I will try not to," she said, parched and weak.

"You will not let it happen again," he said, blue eyes ablaze. "This is an order."

"Yes, Heinrich."

Despite the delay, they arrived at 7:16 am, right on Heinrich's self-imposed schedule. The little red structure reminded Ingrid of the fishing shacks across the harbor back home, where the old men fished and smoked and drank vodka, most eventually having to be fished out themselves after keeling over with their poles in the water. By now, *Mor* and *Far* would have discovered her gone, *Far* likely tearing the apartment apart, while *Mor* followed him from room to room yelling at him to calm down —

The interior was a single room, sparsely furnished with a small dining table, a chair, a metal bed frame with stained mattress without sheets or pillow, an old woodstove with griddle on top, and a sink. There was a toilet in the corner, and a small shower with no curtain. The lone cupboard was filled with two dozen cans of SPAM, a drinking glass, and a corkscrew.

"Perfect," Heinrich said. "We will breakfast, then get some rest. A guest will be arriving in the evening."

"A guest, Heinrich?" Ingrid asked.

"Yes, a Roman Catholic priest. He will wed us and produce an official certificate of marriage authorized by the Vatican."

"But, Heinrich, I am not a Roman Catholic —"

"Not to worry, you will be later this evening."

"But—"

"That is all. Fry some SPAM while I sit on the toilet. This is an order."

That evening, Father-Dr. Carmine Panini—clad in silk suit custom cut by the family tailor in Scoglitti, *cappello romano* atop head, ivory silk collar, pencil mustache that had elicited eye rolls among the more conservative officials at the Rite of Ordination ceremony performed by *Pio XII*—knocked softly on the door of the safehouse, a far cry from his own accommodations in town at the ritzy *Hôtel Eggers*, a profligate lodge of staggering expense.

Uncle Carlo had reached him by telephone at the *Eggers* and explained the situation, which sounded disturbing, but this was family business, and, no matter what *la Famiglia* asked him to do, he could not say no. He knew he had best get used to such interruptions, as they were likely to be frequent in America, where he would be taking over as head of maternity at The Infant Jesus Hospital—"T.I.J.", in Rockville Centre on Long Island, overlooking the Moses-built Southern State Parkway—succeeding the legendary Father-Dr. Napolitano Palermo, who was retiring to Islamorada in the Florida Keys.

The Father-Doctor was expecting a drunken, white-bearded flapdoodle to answer the door, and thus gasped when instead it was a tall, handsome, well-endowed stud with blond hair cropped high and tight and blazing blue eyes, saluting like a man familiar with the joy of discipline—

"I am Captain Heinrich von Schatt," he said in English when he had finished saluting.

Removing his hat, the Father-Doctor, also in English, introduced himself, doing his best to resist the temptation of sneaking a peek at the Captain's crotch. Only Satan could create such a creature, so perfect in appearance, yet the very vision of evil—

"And this is my bride, Ingrid," the Captain said, stepping aside to reveal a pretty brown-haired girl, who looked more like his daughter than his bride—

Inside, next to the bed, Heinrich and Ingrid stood before Father Carmine—

"Before we begin," the Father-Doctor began, "I would like to make sure you both understand the sacrament of marriage under the eyes of God—"

"We understand, Father," Heinrich interrupted. "Now get on with it."

"And you, Ingrid—"

"Get on with it, Father," Heinrich ordered.

When asked if she would take Heinrich as her lawfully wedded husband, Ingrid heard herself say, "I do," then looked at the tattered shade covering the window at the front of the house and saw the silhouette of Uwe Carlsson—

"By the powers vested in me by the Roman Catholic Church," said Father Carmine, "I now pronounce you husband and wife. Captain von Schatt, you may now kiss the bride—"

"Never mind that," Heinrich said. "Where is the certificate?"

"I have it right here," he said, producing the document from his Louis Vuitton satchel.

"Thank you, Father. That will be all. Dismissed."

After Father-Dr. Panini had gone—

"Disrobe for your physical inspection," Heinrich ordered Ingrid.

"Heinrich, what do you mean by *physical inspection*?"

"Wife, I have given you a direct order to disrobe."

"But, Heinrich, I do not understand the purpose of this physical inspection—"

"Wife, I gave you an order!" he roared. "For this insubordination, you have earned ten disciplinary spankings! Disrobe immediately! This is an order!"

While Ingrid was undressing, Heinrich did the same, folding his clothing neatly and placing it on the chair. His thing was large and stiff and pointed towards the ceiling, a shocking sight compared to *Far*'s, which was dainty and pointed towards the floor—

"Bend over the bed," Heinrich ordered. "Palms flat on the mattress."

She obeyed, then heard a *whoosh* just prior to being struck on her bottom, which caused her to bite her lip and draw a trickle of blood. He struck her nine more times, each smack echoing tightly in the room. After he had stopped, she started to stand up straight—

"I have not told you to rise," he said. "Remain as is until I tell you otherwise."

He touched her front private area with his fingers, which was less painful than the spanking, until he tried to squeeze his thing into the tight space. She yelped, but he continued without hesitation. The pain was excruciating and she looked at the window shade, seeing through her tears the silhouette of Uncle Torkel, wanting to cry for him but hardly able to breathe, then everything went dark—

⚓ ⚓ ⚓

At the pier Tuesday evening, right on schedule, Captain Jackbobber Buoy—an American of North African descent, with oversized green teeth and a thick black mustache, his breath a mixture of nicotine, hashish, Scotch whisky, and chocolate—returned Captain von Schatt's salute—

" 'Tis a fine motorcar ya got down in the hold," he said to Heinrich.

"Yes. The Swedes build safe, reliable motorcars. I was advised I would need one in New York."

"Aye, that Moses fella is laying roads like a piper's wife. Do you have a place to stay?"

"No."

"Try Cobble Hill, lots of Swedes there. The butcher, Krög, is always trying to rent out his fancy apartment."

"Where is this Cobble Hill?"

" 'Tis but a taint between the Navy Yard and Red Hook, where we'll be docking."

"The Navy Yard is where they build the ships."

"Aye, they are building 'em faster than they can find coxswains. An experienced one like you should be able to find something over at the Brooklyn Army Terminal. The place is a city within a city. They even have a train depot under a great glass sky. They bring supplies in by rail, then load 'em onto the ships with the soldiers they're sending off to war. Guns, germs, and SPAM, aye."

"This Brooklyn Army Terminal sounds vonderful," Heinrich said, blue eyes ablaze.

"Aye, 'tis a true wonder of the world, Cap'n."

BROOKLYN

1943-1948

Wilma Krög, bored, looking out the window of her father's store—Krög's Butcher Shop on the corner of Court and Dean in Cobble Hill, *Specializing in quality Scandinavian meats since 1928*—had never seen a motorcar like the one that had just pulled up to the curb out front. About to turn thirteen, she had also never seen a man so handsome as the one who emerged from it, who was clearly not from around here, tall with glowing blue eyes and a head of short-cropped blond hair that she thought would look better grown out, and a big bulge in the crotch of his trousers that were hiking them up above his ankles. She was expecting him to pull out a suitcase when he opened the trunk, but, instead, he held out his hand, and out climbed a girl who looked no more than an afternoon or two older than herself.

Through the glass she heard the man order her to get in the car and wait until he returned, to which she replied, "Yes, Heinrich," then scurried into the passenger seat and closed the door. He then looked in Wilma's direction, at the "APARTMENT FOR RENT" sign that her father, Axel, had put in the window, but there were few in these parts who could afford his preposterously high $40-per-month rent, even if it was, as he claimed, "the nicest apartment in the neighborhood", with modern appliances purchased from T.D. Panini & Son—Brooklyn's leading appliance retailer, with locations in Bensonhurst and Canarsie, and coming soon to Ozone Park, Queens.

"What a car!" the butcher said in Swedish, emerging from the back room, white apron freshly bloodied after axing up some reindeer loins. He'd grown up in Östersund and had come to America at the behest of his wife, Hilda, who couldn't bear the thought of spending the rest of her life in that one-moose town, and opened this shop, one of the last on the eastern seaboard still selling reindeer meat post-Depression. "That is a Volvo, from *Sverige*. They build them in *Göteborg*. I have seen them in photographs, but I did not know they are now available in America."

"He's not from America," Wilma said.

"How do you know this, *dotter*?"

"I can just tell. And now here he comes."

The door opened and the little bell jingled. The man stepped inside, causing the daylight filtering into the shop to dim several degrees—

"May I help you?" Axel asked in Swedish, which always annoyed his very American *dotter*.

"I am Captain Heinrich von Schatt," the man said, also in Swedish. "I am here about the apartment for rent."

"You are from *Sverige*?"

"Yes."

"Stockholm? *Göteborg*?"

"*Göteborg*," Heinrich lied. "And you?"

"Östersund. The girl out there—she is your *dotter*?"

"She is my wife."

"Your *fru*? She is just a girl!"

"We have recently wed. I have a Vatican-issued marriage certificate if you must see it."

"Ah. And you are a Captain? What is your ship?"

"I have just arrived and do not yet have a ship, but I will find one promptly at the Brooklyn Army Terminal."

"Ah, I am sure you will, Captain von Schatt, but I am not comfortable renting my apartment to a man not employed —"

"I can pay up front. How much is the rent?"

This is where Axel usually lost prospective tenants with his $40-per-month, but Heinrich agreed to it sight unseen and paid in *kronor* the equivalent of $250 for six months' rent and three pounds of reindeer meat. The butcher handed over the steaks wrapped in heavy brown paper and instructed *dotter* to mind the store while he showed Captain von Schatt upstairs.

The building was three stories—the shop at street level, the Krög apartment on the second floor, and the vacant apartment on the third. At first glance, Heinrich told Krög the apartment would suffice, then dismissed him.

After being retrieved from the car, Ingrid, slightly delirious from Volvo nausea and bouncing around in the trunk, slowly ascended the two flights of stairs fearing that, after the safehouse and *Da Brooklyn Mama*, she was about to walk into yet another den of filth, and was thus surprised when she saw how nice the apartment was, and how clean, and how much bigger it was than the one in Nynäshamn—

"Welcome to our new home, Wife," Heinrich said. "This is how it will be from now on in America, first class, befitting of Captain and Wife."

"Oh, Heinrich, it is beautiful," Ingrid said, and it really was. In the living room, there was a couch and coffee table that looked new, and, in the dining room, a formal dining table with six chairs. In the kitchen, a sea green Bengal gas stove with oven and broiler, a matching sea green Philco refrigerator with built-in freezer compartment, and, on the windowsill above the sink overlooking Dean Street, a sea green, cube-shaped Zenith 5S218 AM/shortwave radio. The drawers were full of utensils, the cabinets full of plates and drinking glasses. In the master bedroom, there was a king-sized bed, and, in the smaller bedroom, a pair of twin beds, all covered with clean sheets, blankets, and pillows. The bathroom had a full-sized claw-foot tub with shower head and a large oval mirror above the sink.

"Tonight, we will feast on reindeer steaks," Heinrich said. "I expect you will have them ready by the time I return this evening. Now I must go find my ship."

Ingrid looked at the Bengal, then back at her husband, wanting to tell him that she'd never used a modern cooking stove like this, but saying instead, "Yes, Heinrich."

⚓　　⚓　　⚓

The Volvo roared down Third Avenue, turning fedora-topped heads along the way, towards the Brooklyn Army Terminal in Sunset Park, encountering at 16th Street the Gowanus Parkway, an elevated thoroughfare, the construction of which, in the signature style of Robert Moses, had torn through residential neighborhoods and displaced thousands of residents—in this case, sections of Finn Town and Little Norway—instead of taking the less destructive route two blocks to the west along the waterfront of crumbling warehouses and rat-infested shipping terminals. At 39th Street, her navigator swung a sharp starboard turn without slowing down, then two blocks later made a hard port side turn onto a set of rusty streetcar tracks embedded into the cobblestones, arriving nearly a mile later at the entrance of the massive 95-acre waterfront military base designed by legendary architect Cass Gilbert, most known for doing the Woolworth Building and celebrated for his rococo style, until Ayn Rand and her raucous band of Frank Lloyd Wright loyalists ridiculed him out of the business.

Inside the grand Warehouse B Atrium, where the midday sun was beaming through the great glass ceiling eight stories above, a freight train was being unloaded by the five-ton moveable crane above the tracks, the cargo being deposited onto beige concrete balconies jutting out from each level like skid row hotels in Old Tangier, then loaded onto the ships docked at the pier. Exiting the atrium, Heinrich crossed a bridge that led him to Pier 3, where two ships bigger than he had ever seen were being loaded. On the lower deck of the pier, supplies were being brought into the cargo holds—guns, tanks, Jeeps, Harley-Davidson motorcycles, medical equipment, towering pallets of SPAM—while, on the upper deck, long lines of uniformed servicemen were smoking the free Lucky Strikes they had just been given while waiting to board the vessels that would bring them to War.

Docked at the far position of Pier 3, was the *USS Flatbush*—one of the newer ships built by the Maritime Commission, the establishment of which by FDR in '42 commenced the frenzy of ship acquisition and building that led to the current glut of vessels and shortage of Captains—a 572-foot transport ship with a Westinghouse geared turbine and twin Foster Wheeler boilers capable of 6,000 shaft horsepower and a top speed of 15.5 knots.

During his reverie, there was a commotion on the gangway when two medics carried a man on a canvas stretcher off the ship and into a waiting ambulance near where Heinrich was standing. They were trailed by four Merchant Marine officers pressing them for more information on his condition, but they would only say they were taking him to St. Albans, the enormous Naval Hospital complex recently built in Queens to accommodate the scores of physically and mentally wounded soldiers being shipped home from the War on a daily basis.

The officers watched helplessly as the vehicle pulled away, which is when the tall man with the blazing blue eyes, clad in foreign Captain's Whites that appeared a couple of sizes short, approached and saluted them. They stared bewilderedly at this gentleman of four outs, none returning his salute—

"What has happened to the man on the stretcher?" Heinrich asked.

"What business is it of yours, bean pole?" one of the officers shot back, flashing angry, ready to scrap.

"He looks like he just stepped out of a Scotch ad," said another.

"Settle down, men," said a mustachioed officer just arrived, older than the other four and with considerably more bars pinned to his uniform coat. Extending his hand to Heinrich, he introduced himself as "Rear Admiral Lower Half Arnold Houlihan, U.S. Merchant Marine."

"Captain Heinrich von Schatt," he said, shaking Houlihan's hand.

"I knew it. I could tell from a mile away you were a Captain."

"That man they carried away—was he Captain of the USS Flatbush?"

"Yes, a relief Captain—Jonas 'Sharky' Waters. He was

relieving another reliever who was reassigned to another ship. Too many goddamn ships and not enough Captains. Where you from, big boy?"

"Sweden. I captained a ferry-ship there."

"A ferry-ship? How long?"

"300 foot. But I can navigate any size vessel, including this one."

"I don't know, son. This mama's nearly twice that size and would tear your little ferry-ship open like a can of muff. But why don't you come to my office and we'll talk some more."

The office was at the old Bush Terminal, the Merchant Marine's own little headquarters adjacent to the BAT. When they arrived, Houlihan led him to a framed photograph on the wall of the *SS Eric Norris*, a 416-foot cargo ship that served in the First Great War and was now being used as a licensing test ship at Fort Wadsworth on Staten Island —

"She's a battered old strumpet, but she's still a good lay," Houlihan said. "Think you can handle her?"

"I can navigate any sea vessel."

"You certainly are a confident son of a bitch."

Houlihan picked up the telephone and arranged for a licensing test on the *Norris*. Half-hour later, after a swift skiff ride across the Upper Bay, Heinrich was at the helm. Despite the subpar condition of the testing ship, and her tendency to slip and jerk, he kept her calm and demonstrated the confidence and control of a seasoned coxswain, perfectly circumnavigating the reeking land mass with impressive precision, then cosseting the old lady to her original position against the Fort Wadsworth pier, earning him a Captain's license and a commission as the new Captain of the *USS Flatbush*, scheduled to depart for Algiers and points beyond the following afternoon at 1600 —

⚓   ⚓   ⚓

Ingrid, monitoring the General Electric wall clock buzzing in the kitchen, pre-heated the oven for exactly ten minutes and cooked the steaks for exactly eight—turning them over after exactly four—and, when she pulled them out, they were succulent. If at that moment her husband had stormed through the door, everything would have worked out perfectly—but he didn't, and the steaks got cold, and an hour went by, then two, and, on two separate occasions when she thought she heard him coming up the stairs, she reheated them for three minutes, which dried them out, so that when he finally did come home, he was unable to cut them, even with the Nobility Lady Empire flatware that had come with the apartment—

"Wife, these steaks are like driftwood," he said, struggling to cut them. He was calm, but Ingrid could tell he was angry. She braced for an eruption, but, instead, without a word, he rose, walked over to the window, opened it, and flung his plate out. There was a brief silence, then the shatter of glazed ceramic upon asphalt, followed by the jangle of cutlery and the dull thud of overcooked reindeer—

"Get undressed for your physical inspection," he said, "and there will be twenty spankings for burning my steaks."

A floor below, Wilma Krög, in nightgown and socks, crawled out her bedroom window onto the fire escape. She climbed the narrow iron steps to her perch just left of the third floor living room window, where she could see inside through a small space she had fashioned in the curtain when the apartment was vacant, making a tiny fold in the fabric just wide enough to see into the room, yet subtle enough that no one had ever noticed it. Her eye widened at seeing the girl bent over the couch being spanked, then widened further when Captain von Schatt stuck his giant thing in her *from behind*. That lasted a few seconds before the Captain grunted and pulled out, then suddenly turned towards the window as if he knew she was there, his blazing blue eyes seemingly looking right at her through the space in the curtain, his giant dripping thing facing her like a saber. For the first time ever during one of her fire escape missions, she panicked, nearly falling several times as she rushed down the shaking stairs and dove through the open window onto her bed —

The following afternoon, Ingrid, still lightheaded after feeling faint on the subway ride to the Brooklyn Army Terminal, scurried to keep up with Heinrich as he steamed through the atrium, then across the bridge onto Pier 3. In his gleaming new Captain's Whites that the ladies in the Bush Terminal tailor shop had spent all night putting together and messengered to the apartment earlier that morning, Heinrich stopped at a spot ten yards in front of the gangway —

"This exact spot is where you will wait to greet me for arrivals, and send me off for departures," he said. "For departures, you will remain in this spot saluting after the *Flatbush* has departed, until she is no longer visible on the horizon. For arrivals, you must be here saluting two hours before the official scheduled arrival time, and hold your salute until I have disembarked the vessel and saluted in return. Is this understood?"

"Yes, Heinrich."

Heinrich quick-saluted her, then, after a sharp 180-degree pivot, headed up the gangway and disappeared into the ship.

Passersby had slowed to witness the spectacle, while Rear Admiral Lower Half Houlihan, having seen this sort of thing before with Captains, had a team of medics on standby over the next several hours in case she went down, but she did not, holding her salute until the *Flatbush* disappeared beyond the Narrows—

⚓   ⚓   ⚓

Beyond Algiers, Heinrich's initial voyage on the *Flatbush* continued east to Bizerte, across the Mediterranean, through the Suez Canal, down the formerly Moses-parted Red Sea, and across the Arabian to Bombay, before turning around and heading back west, making stops at Oran and Liverpool, and, finally, crossing the Atlantic on the same course as Captain Smith on the *Titanic*, getting near as he could to the coordinates without compromising the schedule, hoping to see something, but finding the horizon dark—

Four days before Christmas, alone in America for the past three months, having ventured no further than the butcher shop downstairs and the little grocery store up the street that she didn't like because it made her think of home, the Western Union man finally delivered the telegram Ingrid had been awaiting—

> USS FLATBUSH ARRIVING 24 DECEMBER 1600 HOURS BROOKLYN ARMY TERMINAL PIER 3 BE AT SPOT BY 1400 HOURS TAKE NUMBER 2 SUBWAY CAPT VON SCHATT

Two months earlier, realizing that, since arriving in America, she hadn't had the bleeding, which had only just begun less than a year ago, she telephoned Father-Dr. Panini and he arranged to have a car drive her to The Infant Jesus Hospital out on Long Island for an examination. Three weeks later, he called back with the results, confirming that she was with child, due between May and September.

She decided she would tell Heinrich after serving his homecoming meal, which she wrote out a plan for. Upon their return from the pier, she would invite him to sit at the dining table and serve him *Wasabröd* with thinly sliced *Västerbotten* cheese and a glass of *Whesskey*. While he was busy with that, she would quickly heat up the meatballs cooked earlier that morning, and put the already-seasoned-and-marinated reindeer steaks in the broiler to be ready by the time he finished the meatballs. For dessert, coffee and *butterkaka*, which is when she would break the news—

On Christmas Eve, three hours before the *Flatbush* was due, she set out in the chilly, overcast afternoon, making the mile-long walk to the Atlantic Avenue terminal, where she boarded a #2 subway towards 59th Street in Sunset Park—just as she had practiced three times a week, in addition to her daily saluting drills. Today, though, she started having brief blackouts on the train, which hadn't happened during the practice runs. Then she had a long one and missed her stop, finally regaining consciousness at 77th Street, where she had to get on another train back to 59th. The atrium was dim and cold, and a whipping breeze was swirling off the Upper Bay as she arrived at the spot on Pier 3, early enough that she was in position and saluting properly upon coming into view of Heinrich's military grade Bausch & Lomb binoculars—

Wilma Krög, at her window overlooking Dean Street, tossed aside the Christmas issue of *Calling All Girls* when she saw Captain von Schatt materialize in a cone of streetlamp light up the block, followed by his girl-wife. Since panicking on the fire escape several months earlier, she had been angry with herself and longing for his return so she could look right into his bright blue eyes, but, as they approached the building, he did not look up in her direction. After they had disappeared inside, she grabbed her Eastman Kodak Baby Brownie camera and ascended the fire escape stairs—

When they arrived home, Ingrid invited Heinrich to sit, then placed the *Wasabröd, Västerbotten,* and *Whesskey* on the table. After he was seated, she put the meatballs in the oven and pre-heated the broiler for the steaks. When he'd finished the first course, she poured him another *Whesskey* and served the meatballs, then put the steaks in the broiler, flipping them after four minutes and leaving them in for another four. When she took them out they were succulent, and she hoped he would say something complimentary when she placed the plate in front of him, but he remained silent, not even glancing up at her, and she began to worry she had done something wrong—down in the butcher shop yesterday, the Krög girl did seem to find it humorous that she would be serving reindeer on Christmas Eve. She watched him pick up his fork and knife and cut a piece that appeared too large, but he put it in his mouth anyway, breathing loudly through his nose and grunting as he chewed. She sat and started cutting her own steak, tempted to ask if he liked his but afraid of interrupting, so she waited until the last morsel was gone and the chewing noises had stopped—

"Heinrich, how did you like the steaks?"

"The steaks were satisfactory, Wife," he said, using the cloth napkin to wipe a drop of meat juice from his chin.

"Oh, I am happy to hear this. Now I will get the coffee and *butterkaka,* and I have some wonderful news to tell you."

After lighting a Pall Mall, he called into the kitchen, "What is this vonderful news you speak of?"

Ingrid waited until she returned to the table and was

placing cup, saucer, and *butterkaka* in front of him before answering, "I was not feeling so well a few weeks after you left, so I called Father-Doctor Panini and explained my symptoms. He sent a car that took me to his hospital on Long Island—"

"He sent a car?"

"Yes, Heinrich."

"What kind of car?"

"It was a Cadillac."

"A fine American automobile. Proceed."

"The Father-Doctor gave me an examination—"

"What type of examination?"

"A with-child examination."

"And what were the results of this with-child examination?"

"I am with child."

"A masculine child, I presume," he said, exhaling while stamping out his cigarette. "We will name him 'Heinrich von Schatt II'."

She looked at him, wanting to tell him that this was God's decision, but afraid of upsetting him—

"Yes, Heinrich," she said.

⚓   ⚓   ⚓

In the hours before dawn on 6 June 1944, in less than ideal weather conditions, General Dwight D. Eisenhower, too antsy to wait another month for the next full moon, commenced Operation Overlord, and a thousand Allied warplanes swarmed across the English Channel towards Normandy—

Meanwhile, in Brooklyn, Ingrid, alone with the moon and the child being born, was hunched over the telephone table in the hallway waiting for the operator to make the connections to The Infant Jesus Hospital, legs pressed together, a trail of drops marking her journey from the puddle of amniotic fluid in the kitchen, Heinrich out at sea for another week—

"The Father-Doctor has gone home for the evening," said Sister Enid after the connection was made, "but stay on the line and I will attempt to contact him."

On Woodland Drive, in his home just beyond the hospital parking lot, the Father-Dr., glass of *Panini Nero d'Avola* in hand, had just gotten comfortable on the leather couch after flicking on the home film projector, looking forward to finally screening the reel he had recently purchased from a man in a trenchcoat on 42nd Street, *YMCA After Dark*, when the telephone rang, prompting a Heavenward roll of the eyes before stopping the projector and approaching the ringing nuisance down the hall. After Sister Enid explained the situation, he called his sixth-cousin Vito at the cab stand in Brooklyn, asking him to send the Cadillac to pick up Mrs. von Schatt in Lynbrook and bring her to Rockville Centre—

An hour later, sprawled on the springy back seat of a Cadillac racing east on the Belt Parkway, the cabin thick with cigar smoke, Ingrid blacked out. It would be hours before she regained consciousness, opening her eyes to a pair of iron-rimmed glasses attempting to hand her a baby wrapped in a blanket—

"What is this?" she asked, trying to back away—

"It is your child," said Sister Enid.

"Congratulations, Mrs. von Schatt!" smiled Father-Doctor Panini, peeking over Sister Enid's shoulder—

"Oh, dear," Ingrid said, "please let this be a masculine child—"

"It is a feminine child," Sister Enid reported. "Her soul is dim, otherwise, she is healthy. Would you like to hold her?"

Ingrid looked away and blacked out again. She was still out the following morning, during Sister Golden Hair's shift—

"Ilsa," said Ingrid, in a colorless dream that she was on a dark tarmac following Ilsa Lund towards a waiting plane being piloted by a blond-haired man in a lab coat—

"I beg your pardon, Mrs. von Schatt?"

"Ilsa—"

"No, Mrs. von Schatt. I am Sister Golden Hair."

"Ilsa—"

"Oh, *now* I understand! Ilsa is a beautiful name!"

The next morning, Father-Doctor Panini telephoned Rear Admiral Lower Half Houlihan, who telegraphed a message to the *Flatbush* congratulating Captain von Schatt on the birth of his daughter, Ilsa von Schatt, 8 lbs 6 oz—

One week later, mother and daughter still at the hospital, the baby's evening feeding was interrupted by the roar of a car engine outside, at first far off in the distance, but continuing to grow louder, until it finally stopped just outside the building—

Father-Dr. Panini—who had sent a truckload of high-end baby gifts to the apartment, including Taylor Tot stroller, Kiddie-Koop combo Crib / Play Pen / Bassinet, sterling silver Tiffany rattle, two dozen cases of disposable silk diapers from Doyers Street in Chinatown, and all manners of blankets, nursing bottles, and promotional feminine hygiene samples sent to TIJ Maternity on a daily basis—was in his office enjoying a Benson & Hedges when he heard Captain von Schatt roar into the lobby demanding to know where his wife was, then, without awaiting a response, begin opening and slamming shut the doors of the patient rooms until he found the right one—

"Heinrich!" exclaimed Ingrid, as the baby attempted to bury her head in her *Mor*'s breast—

"God damn it, Wife!" he roared, slapping the now-wrinkled paper with the telegraph message he'd received on the *Flatbush*, which he let fall and blanket the baby's head. "I demanded a masculine child!"

"But, Heinrich, isn't she beautiful?"

"Next time I expect a son! This is an order!"

⚓ ⚓ ⚓

Two-and-a-half years later, despite routine physical inspections during Heinrich's homecomings, Ingrid had yet to experience any signs of being with child anew—

It was Thanksgiving Eve, 1946, the War over, and Ilsa, bored, tossed aside her doll after hearing the promotional announcement on radio 570 WMCA for Macy's, where Santa would be floating in at the end of the Thanksgiving Day parade the next morning, then, starting Friday, would be stationed on the tenth floor of the store—

"Tomorrow you will take me to Macy's," said the girl, blue eyes ablaze, to her *Mor*. "That's an order."

"Yes, Ilsa," Ingrid said.

Winter arrived the next morning, 23° when *Mor* and *dotter* set out for R. H. Macy & Company, boarding a Manhattan-bound #2 BMT Broadway Local. The girl had inherited a dose of her *Far*'s navigational skills and already knew her way around the subways, so, except for Ingrid having a couple of minor blackouts in the air pressure changes below the East River, they arrived without incident at the 34th Street-Herald Square station.

Up on the street, smells of hot pretzels, roasted chestnuts, perfume, and tobacco smoke swirled in the cold air, while taxis honked and handsomely-attired families packed the sidewalks, the men wearing suits, the ladies wearing long fur coats and bright red lipstick, the children dressed in their Sunday suits and dresses. Through the revolving doors they were whisked into the warm grandeur of the world's largest department store—co-founded by Isidor Straus, who, with his beloved wife, Ida, died on the *RMS Titanic*, she refusing to jump in the lifeboat without him—

Ilsa wanted to go to the jewelry counter, but ladies in green elf costumes were directing the droves of arriving families up the escalator to the fourth floor, the end of the line to see Santa up on the tenth. For six hours, they inched their way up the steps of the motionless escalators, which had been turned off to accommodate the slow-moving line, Ilsa peeing in her underpants twice, and Ingrid once, as had most of the mothers without husbands who'd refused to surrender their place in line to go down to the basement and the only ladies' room in the store not out of service, which itself had a three-hour wait, leaving the upper levels of the store pungently humid as the end of an August doubleheader at Ebbets Field.

At one point, Ilsa turned around to discover a slightly older boy standing uncomfortably close to her with a pair of leather aviation goggles strapped around his head and an extra-wide smile exposing crooked teeth and hot onion breath, urine streaks running down the insides of his oversaturated trouser legs dripping yellow at the cuffs—

"I like *The Wizard of Oz*," he said, his dried lips sticking to his gums like a horse-toothed jackass. "I like Uncle Henry."

"You're gross," Ilsa said.

"Santa can hear you."

"You'll die poor."

Finally, on the tenth floor, Ilsa was hoisted by two lady-elves onto Santa's lap, prompting her to scream just in time for the popping flashbulb of the Polaroid Magic Camera that produced photographic prints in sixty seconds—

"And what is your name, little girl?" Santa asked the scowling child, who did not answer—

"Her name is Ilsa," Ingrid finally said.

"So, Ilsa, what would you like for Christmas?"

Ilsa did not answer.

"She wants a Dala horse," Ingrid eventually said.

"She wants a horse?"

"A Dala horse. It is a little wooden toy."

"Do you live on a farm?"

"Never mind the dumb horse," Ilsa finally said. "I want jewelry. Diamonds and emeralds in all shapes and sizes, gold and pearls and sparkling surprises, or I'm going to scream."

Santa motioned Ingrid to lean in. As she did, she caught a whiff of what smelled like Heinrich's *Whesskey*—

"You should head up to Bloomingdale's," he said, quietly. "They have nicer stuff up there and it actually costs a little less. Here they'll rob you blind with the markup that pays for all the goddamn parades and fireworks. And if you're interested in an evening of romance, meet me at Loading Dock C at 10:15, which is over on the 35th Street side. Just be careful of the muggers, it's dark back there that time of night."

"Take me to Bloomingdales," Ilsa said to *Mor*. "That's an order."

"You've got a Bloomie on your hands, heh, heh—I mean, ho-ho," Santa winked. "She'll like it better than this shithole. It smells like the men's room at Aqueduct in here, except without all the old queers."

"Print ready!" the camera elf called, dangling the

photograph of Ilsa screaming on Santa's lap. "That'll be two dollars."

"Oh, no thank you," Ingrid said, unaware that a photograph had even been taken, having momentarily blacked out when the bulb flashed.

"Not a choice, ma'am. Mandatory. Two dollars or else I'm gonna have to call security. And the cells down in the basement are already mighty crowded. Lots of deadbeats today. If we keep sending them down, they might have to start shipping them up to Rikers."

Finally, after paying the two dollars and being released by the elves, they were back outside, the cold air refreshing after the Macy's schvitz. They headed east, then turned uptown at Fifth Avenue, where lavish window displays depicted scenes of the modern American Christmas—well-attired father mannequins smoking pipes in front of fireplaces as wife and children mannequins looked on adoringly, mustachioed snowmen modeling argyle sweater-vests and derby hats, Lionel electric trains lapping Christmas trees, Daisy Red Ryder air rifles pointing at taxidermized bear cubs, dolls in ball gowns gossiping around a punch bowl filled with red-Jell-O. North of 42nd Street, diamonds started appearing in the windows, and, up near Central Park, horse-drawn carriages were being navigated by top-hatted Dickensian buggy Captains, while enormous Cadillac limousines deftly swerved around piles of manure. At 59th Street, Ilsa pointed at The Plaza and said she wanted to live there, but Ingrid was unresponsive, pulling the girl east across Madison, Park, and Lexington, until they were sucked into another revolving door that this time brought them into the brilliant glare of fluorescent light upon highly-buffed white linoleum, blinding them to all but the golden angels soaring above them leaving faerie dust in their wakes, the only sounds the gentle murmur of browsers and the soft strum of an unseen harp. It took a moment for the girl's eyes to adjust to the brilliance, the scene fading in like a print from the Magic Camera. She saw first the sparkle of the jewelry counter, then the fancy ladies seated in high-backed chairs sampling the latest lipstick shades, then other ladies sniffing their inner wrists at the perfume counter, and, throughout the floor, the white-gloved attendants subtly watching the clientele, ready to pounce at the first sign of assistance needed. No long lines here, no waiting hours on a motionless escalator with the proletariat and their urine-soaked urchins, just the hushed tones of wealth whispering in a young girl's ear—

⚓   ⚓   ⚓

Fourth of July, 1947, Wilma Krög bopping down the Coney Island boardwalk as if her mother hadn't died a month ago, the morning breeze already delivering smells of hot dogs, popcorn, cotton candy, Rheingold Extra Dry, seaweed, raw sewage, and vomit—the latter especially pungent near the Cyclone. She spent a dime to watch The Mighty Ajax swallow a sword, and someone in the crowd called him a "fake"— which she already knew was part of the act, one of Ajax's guys, a derby-hatted gentleman named Vermin planted in the audience, and Ajax would, of course, win the man over with his amazing natural gifts. Shows later in the day would end with a rousing ovation, but, at this morning hour, as the boardwalk shook off its daily hangover, there was only a smattering of applause, the early crowds a long way from Chinese firecrackers after sunset. Afterwards, she stopped to watch Woody the Guitar-Man with hand-painted placard glued crookedly to his instrument that said *THIS MACHINE KILLS FASCISTS*, playing a sub-subversive sub verse of his crowd-pleasing "This Land Is Your Land", which he'd been playing for over an hour now and was on his 73rd unique lyric—

The girls work without representation
In back alleys near Penn Station
These girls should organize their occupation
This land was made for you and me

The Captain would be home later that afternoon, Wilma knew, having the day before overheard the girl-wife in the shop ordering reindeer steaks, which always meant he was due at port the next day. In her pocket she had some cash pilfered from the Krög's Butcher Shop till that she used to buy a pink bikini with black polka dots at *Zezette's Beach Couture*, a small shop sandwiched between *Madame Bouvier's House of Burlesque* and the ramshackle theater that hosted Wanda the Turtle Girl, portrayed on the placard as a young lady on all fours with a giant turtle shell on her back.

After five hot dogs and three Coca-Colas at Nathan's, she went home and changed into her new bikini, then set up camp on the roof, which smelled strongly of hot tar, one of her favorite scents. When she was little and not yet old enough to hate her parents, they used to eat dinner up here as a family in the last of the summer daylight, after the store had been locked up for the night. Now, in his permanent depression since Mother died, Father hardly ever left the store, and, unable to bear the thought of sleeping in their old bed without her, had converted the little storage room into a den with a cot, reading chair, and radio, and had a shower installed in the shop bathroom. Thus, he did not see his daughter, clad in triangular slivers of polka-dotted fabric, climb the stairs to the roof with a pitcher of iced lemonade, two glasses, a pack of Camels, a matchbook from the Hot Rod Hotel, a souvenir Wonder Wheel ashtray, and a pair of pink *Nancy Drew Lady Detective* binoculars she had stolen from her friend, Betty-Lou.

She moved the wrought iron mesh-top patio table and one of the chairs into the trapezoid of shade provided by the staircase doorway housing, then, over the next several hours, smoked cigarettes and drank lemonade while staking out Dean Street, until her eye finally caught the gleam of Captain's Whites in the late afternoon sun. After refilling her glass, she brought it over to the waist-high roof wall and posed with it until he noticed, prompting him to turn around and order the girl-wife and daughter to look down at the sidewalk while they ambulated. After they had complied, he looked up again, blue eyes ablaze, trousers hitched, until arriving at the building, when, just before stepping inside, the little girl looked up and saw their near-nude neighbor, beverage in hand, leaning over the wall watching them—

Heinrich, after being greeted at the pier by Wife and girl-child, was leading them down the last stretch of the mile-long walk home from the Atlantic Avenue subway terminal, when he spied movement atop the apartment building. It was the butcher's daughter, visible from the waist up behind the rooftop wall, beverage in hand, clad in a pair of triangular fabric slices that hardly concealed her breasts, which had grown considerably since the last time he'd seen her—

"The butcher girl is a woman now," he said out loud to himself, then turned and ordered Wife and girl-child to look down at the sidewalk while they ambulated.

Inside the building, he stopped them just outside their

apartment door—

"Tonight's physical inspection will be postponed until tomorrow evening," he said to Ingrid. "Right now, you and the girl-child will go inside and have supper on the table in exactly fifteen minutes. Do not leave the apartment or answer the door, unless it is I, your Captain. This is an order."

"Yes, Heinrich."

Up on the roof, Wilma started trembling after hearing the apartment door close down below, then the Captain's footsteps scraping up the stairs—

"Lemonade?" she asked as he stepped through the doorway, offering the glass—

"Yes, thank you," he said, accepting the refreshment.

"Do you like my bikini *couture*?"

"It is vonderful," he said, raising glass to lips without taking his eyes off her body.

"I'm ready for my spankings and physical inspection," she said, but it came out too soft and coincided with him putting glass to lips and draining the contents in one long sip, so she wasn't sure if he'd heard and couldn't decide if she should repeat herself. By the time he placed the empty glass down on the table, her thought process had dissolved without arriving at a decision, then he stared at her without saying anything, which both frightened and excited her—

"Remove your *couture*," he finally said.

As she removed her bikini top and bottom, she allowed him a moment to inspect her recently thickened bush that had filled in nicely during the unseasonably warm spring, which she had not been shy about showing off to the other girls at school with their pathetic little weed patches. After draping the bikini pieces over the back of the chair, she bent over the table the same way she had so many times seen the girl-wife bent over the back of their living room couch, then waited. When at first he did not move, she began to fear that he had changed his mind, until finally she heard him unbuckle his belt, slip off his shoes, and remove his trousers, which he folded neatly and placed on the table between her hands. She tried to get a peek at his thing, but it was covered by the curtain of his uniform shirt, which he did not remove. After he had positioned himself behind her, she was too afraid to turn and look directly at him, focusing instead on the folded trousers, briefs, and neatly rolled white leather belt in front of her. Then, suddenly, her bottom was stung by his open hand, and again nine more times, before he forced his giant thing into her tight space, and, finally, she cried for Mother—

⚓   ⚓   ⚓

The green awning was gone and everything around it had changed, but the building that once housed the Sisters of Mercy Orphanage Bremerhaven Ancillary Location was still there, having survived Allied bombing during the War, and looking otherwise as it had on Christmas Eve, 1936, the last time Heinrich had been here. He was unaware of what had transpired after his flight to Sweden—Hosenpinkel killing six Nazis in the harbor, prompting a brutal crackdown led by General Streck of the High Command, who claimed the Sisters of Mercy building for his local headquarters, then ordered his men to shoot the nuns and orphans and burn their bodies in the basement furnace—and, only five years ago, it was inconceivable that he'd ever set foot in his childhood city again. Yet, on this gray January day in 1948, Captain Heinrich von Schatt once more approached the steps on which he'd been left as a newborn, in front of which now stood an

American soldier on guard, whom he saluted, and whom returned the salute. The building was now being used as administrative offices by the Allies, who had rebuilt the port into a massive complex to accommodate the influx of soldiers they were sending all over Europe to keep an eye on the Soviets, leaving no remnants of his tiny old pier.

The lobby had been renovated, but the corridor leading to his former quarters in the Isolated Wing looked the same. His old door was unlocked, the room filled with boxes of paperwork. He found none of his old wall markings, or any other sign that the space had been his. At the window, still caged, the old view now obstructed by Allied dormitory buildings, he retrieved from the tiny crack between cage and sill a slip of folded stationery, on which was written with dripping quill, *42°6'6.6"N 48°6'6.6"W*—

Afterwards, he walked up the *Barkhausenstraße*, to the twin apartment buildings, and into the courtyard where it happened. The space seemed smaller in the gray light, but the stack of trash cartons in the corner looked the same. He briefly considered moving them to see if there was a skeleton beneath, but he didn't want to soil his Captain's Whites, so he instead headed back to the pier, where someone was calling in German, "Captain, Captain, over here, Captain..."

The old man, very old now, was seated on a wooden chair behind a small folding table, on top of which were two mechanical devices with red and black wires hanging out of their back sides.

"You look like a man who appreciates precision engineering," he said.

"This is true," Heinrich said. "These devices—are they transistor radios?"

"No. They are electric can openers manufactured by the

Third Reich. I found them at a bombed-out factory in Schiffdorf. These are the last two."

"Intriguing," Heinrich said, picking one up. "How does it work?"

"You install it on your kitchen wall," the old man said, picking up a can of *jagdwurst* and demonstrating how the lid fit into the wheel. "As you can see, this part looks like a regular old manual can opener—but, when you push down the handle like this, the can automatically spins around, and the cutting disc slices the lid perfectly without all the jagged edges, and there is a magnet that catches it for easy disposal. It has a 2-horsepower motor hardwired into the house's electricity. There is no effort required on your part besides holding the can beneath it and pushing down the handle. A child could operate it."

"What a vonderful device," Heinrich said.

"So, would you like to purchase one? It is ten American dollars."

"I will purchase both," Heinrich said.

Five nights later, on the Bridge of the USS *Flatbush*, near the coordinates, Heinrich, after years of Atlantic crossings, finally spied something through his Bausch & Lombs, a faint red glow to the north beyond the icefield, accompanied by a chorus of low, hardly audible moans that were causing the helm knobs to vibrate—

LYNBROOK

1948–1960

It was 12° Fahrenheit on that Tuesday afternoon in February 1948, but Heinrich, with an electric can opener in each hand, was wearing a short-sleeve plaid button-down shirt tucked into a pair of Captain's Casuals khaki trousers as he stood on the frozen dust of one of the two 5,000 square-foot lots he'd bought out on Long Island, this one in Lynbrook, the other in the neighboring village of Valley Stream, both purchased through southwestern Nassau County's premier real estate broker, Pasquale Andrea Panini Jr. III, who was late again, just as he'd been for the closings back in December. While waiting, Heinrich smoked an entire Pall Mall without removing it from his lips, watching a crane over at the construction site a block down and across the confounding five-way asterisk-shaped intersection formed by Hendrickson Avenue, Franklin Avenue, South Franklin Avenue, and two separate, misaligned sections of Hempstead Avenue. They were building a modern new shopping center to be anchored by Dan's Foods, the crane slowly hoisting one of two enormous "DAN'S FOODS" neon signs atop a hundred-foot tall brick monolith that looked like a flattened chimney, which, in the dark Lynbrook night, would glow red and blink a repeating pattern until the store opened at dawn. Dan, known by his associates as "The Man", had initially preferred a Jones Beach-style Italianate obelisk that would enable them to put signs up facing all four horizons, but cost overruns forced them to scale back and instead go with a monolith that could accommodate only two neon signs, one facing East towards Montauk, and the other West towards the city. At dusk, the signs would flicker on, dim at first, but, after a few minutes, they would warm to their full brilliance and could be seen from every backyard in the eastern and western sections of North Lynbrook and the southwest quadrant of Malverne. At night, the monolith couldn't be seen against the dark sky, making the fifteen-foot tubular letters appear to be hovering, which would result in Lynbrook becoming a global hotspot for flying saucer sightings. The store name was broken into two lines— *DAN'S* on the first line, *FOODS* on the second, programmed with a timing mechanism that would illuminate one letter at a time—D-A-N-'-S F-O-O-D-S—then all the letters would blink slowly in unison three times—DAN'S FOODS / DAN'S FOODS / DAN'S FOODS—and then blink six times really fast—DAN'S FOODS DAN'S FOODS DAN'S FOODS DAN'S FOODS DAN'S FOODS DAN'S FOODS—before going dark and starting over again ten seconds later. The shopping center would also be home to Nelson's Barber Shop, Stella's Beauty Parlor, Guy John Jr.'s Men's Shoes Sales & Repair, the United States Armed Forces Recruiting Station, Lynbrook Savings and Loan, Ruth's Flower Shop, Ralph's Appliance Repair & Service, Lefty's Liquors and Wine, The Stationery Store, an ancillary station of the Lynbrook post office, The Best Great Wall Chinese Food Restaurant Takeout Laundry, and The Law Office of Saul Rosenblatt, Esq.

Several minutes later, Pasquale's black Cadillac Series 62 finally pulled up next to the curb, and the generously proportioned figure, in brown mink overcoat and matching mink bomber hat, emerged from the vehicle.

"Jesus fuckin' Christ," he called, waddling towards Heinrich, cigar in hand. "Aren't you cold dressed like that?"

"You are tardy, and I am not cold," Heinrich said. "Why are there men working over there and not here?"

"The ground's been frozen since you purchased the lot, so we haven't been able to pour the foundation. They started working on the shopping center last spring, so their foundations are already dug and poured, and now all the work is above ground. Whatcha got there, radios?"

"These are electric can openers. I would like one hardwired into the electric system in the Galley of each house."

"Electric can openers?" Pasquale chuckled. "To open your cans of spinach?"

"What is this about spinach?"

"You know, you're a Captain, and Popeye was a sailor who ate canned spinach and grew big musk-els, ah-guh-guh-guh—"

"I will throw this sailor in the brig if he ever sets foot on my ship."

"Yes, well, I'll give those can openers to the foreman at each site, no problem at all. We appreciate the business, Captain von Schatt."

Normally, the Panini crews used their own suppliers, but Heinrich had already purchased two truckloads of surplus shipbuilding materials at a deep discount from the Brooklyn Navy Yard, which, with the Maritime Commission in the process of culling its aging ships from a fleet that had become bloated during the War, had shifted its focus from building ships to scrapping them. He also commissioned a freelance architect—a young guy named Pei, who had been at the

Brooklyn Army Terminal with his Kodak studying the work of Cass Gilbert during an arrival of the *USS Flatbush*, and who had the misfortune of unwittingly positioning himself on Pier 3 in the wrong place at the wrong time and getting run over by a blur of white, busting his favorite lens—to design a "ship-house" based on the procured materials from the Navy Yard, which would be used to build identical structures on both the Lynbrook and Valley Stream lots.

Heinrich also commissioned Norman, the curly-headed kid who was always hanging around the pier with his easel and palette making paintings of the ships that he would sell for a quarter each, to paint two identical portraits depicting Heinrich as a giant, godlike figure in his Captain's Whites, standing behind the horizon watching the *USS Flatbush* navigate the angry Atlantic. The boy suggested some hopeful white clouds with happy rays of sun bursting through with God's joy, but this angered Heinrich, who demanded a foreboding sky and seething whitecaps—

Pei, frustrated that his early drafts looked like little tugboat-houses instead of the mighty ship-house Captain von Schatt demanded, eventually came up with a design that made the structure look like the bridge housing of a large ship protruding from the ground, implying that the rest of the ship was buried beneath. It would be a ranch with 900 square feet on the main floor and 450 square feet of finished basement, and another 450 for the boiler/laundry/storage room. There would be a gangway leading to the front door, and a thirty-foot high flagpole in the front yard with Old Glory up top. The house exterior would be covered with flame-retardant asbestos shingles triple-coated with Pittsburgh Paints Captain's White, as would the detached garage in the southeast corner of the lot at the end of the driveway. Inside the garage, there would be room enough for the Volvo and, in the back, a small, enclosed workshop filled with Sears Craftsman tools, the room accessible through a side door facing the backyard. The yard would be a rectangle of dust seeded with tall fescue that would fail to take root and morph into a network of tangled crabgrass that would never need mowing. A concrete patio would extend from the back of the house and be covered by a green-and-white-striped canvas awning supported by a framework of steel pipes footed in the concrete and attached to the house beneath the gutter, creating an outdoor living space furnished with picnic table and several pastel blue and green rubber-strap Gulfstream pool chairs, and, next to each, a small round table with frosted glass and white plastic ashtrays. Even during summer showers, the family could dine out of doors and enjoy the falling rain, unless there was lightning, when a direct strike on the piping would turn the space into something resembling a Tesla experiment.

A three-step brick stoop would lead up to the back door and into the Galley loaded with appliances from T.D. Panini & Son, including sea green Philco refrigerator and Bengal gas stove like the ones in Cobble Hill. A vinyl asbestos composite with mini-redbrick pattern would cover the Galley and all floors on the port side of the house. The countertops would be covered with PPG Captain's White formica speckled with decorative gold flake. Above the counters would be tall sheet metal cabinets, also PPG Captain's White, that rumbled like thunder whenever anyone opened or closed them. The stainless-steel sink would be illuminated by a buzzing track of miniature fluorescent tube lighting beneath the short cabinet above the sink. The main Galley light would be a larger buzzing fluorescent tube up on the middle of the ceiling.

Across from the sink, against the wall, would be a small dining table also with gold flaked formica, and, docked on the three open sides, metal-framed chairs upholstered with Dow Chemical *Plasticizer 6000* vinyl in seafoam green. The electric can opener would be installed on the wall next to the back door at the height of the Captain's breast, red and black wires spliced into the house circuitry, its chrome arm shining in the fluorescence ready to be pushed down onto the little black button that would set the 2-horsepower motor into motion and sound like a city bus roaring through the tiny Galley. A swinging door would lead to the CAPTAIN'S MESS—the formal dining room—and a regular door with LOWER DECK in gold leaf would lead to *"the basement staircase"*, as Pei referred to it in his personal notes, but not on the blueprints, correctly assuming the non-nautical reference would upset Captain von Schatt.

The Captain's Mess would be furnished with a handcrafted stained oak dining table surrounded by overstuffed chairs, Heinrich having instructed the designers to mimic Captain Smith's Mess on the RMS *Titanic*. Openly adjoining the Captain's Mess would be the CAPTAIN'S LOUNGE—the living room—covered with plush wall-to-wall Captain's White carpeting that anyone other than Heinrich was forbidden to tread upon, and furnished with Captain's White post-Victorian-pre-modern-post-War sofa and sitting chairs, all permanently covered with clear plastic. Facing the bow, three bay-bridge windows would overlook the front yard and Hendrickson Avenue.

On the port side of the house, there would be a short corridor leading to the CREW LOUNGE, HEAD, CAPTAIN'S QUARTERS, and a small, unnamed bedroom. The Crew Lounge would be a tiny den, where, on the wall above the wood-framed loveseat with leather cushions, the commissioned painting would hang, the eyes blazing blue and following anyone who entered the room. Directly across from the loveseat stood an odd-looking monolithic object about three-foot high made of dark wood with a piece of curved glass towards the top that looked like a blank face—the salesman at T. D. Panini & Son called it a *"television set"* and described it as *"a personal cinema for the modern home"*, this one a full-size Admiral Wonder console with 30 tube chassis and a 61-square inch viewing screen. Next door to the Crew Lounge would be the Captain's Quarters, as indicated with extra-large gold leaf with double-bold black outline on the door, and furnished with a "Captain's Size" bed that was the next size up from a king. The unnamed bedroom at the end of the hall would be Ilsa's, and there would be no gold leaf, or any lettering, on her door.

As on most seafaring vessels, interior space was limited—therefore, the Lower Deck staircase would be extra-narrow, somewhere between standard basement staircase and fire escape. Individuals with generously proportioned feet would have to descend sideways and ascend on their toes, and each step would be covered with black linoleum impossible to see with the lights off, the only visual marker being strips of grooved aluminum nailed to the edge of each step to prevent slippage. Even seasoned seamen accustomed to narrow nautical steps would not expect to find such a staircase in a suburban home, especially this far out on Long Island.

At the bottom of the stairs, immediately to the right, would be the quarters reserved for the FIRST MALE HEIR—smaller gold leaf on the door, medium bold black outline—and, to the left, the large open space of the OFFICERS' LOUNGE, the floors covered with highly-buffed black linoleum that extended into the FIRST MALE HEIR's quarters, and the walls covered with dark lacquered wood panels adorned with nautical memorabilia, which, in the Lynbrook house, would include the original helm of the *USS Flatbush*, and a white life preserver customized with hand-painted "Heinrich von Schatt" arcing across the top and "Captain" arcing across the bottom. The space would be furnished with black leather couch, oak coffee table, and a pair of matching sitting chairs flanked by FDR-era sand-filled standup brass ashtrays. The linoleum would gleam brilliantly under the sharp buzzing track of fluorescent tube lighting built into the mentholated asbestos ceiling panels. At the far end of the space would be a head with black toilet and rumbling sheet metal shower stall that, when in use, rumbled like an August afternoon thunderboomer in Islamorada. The ENGINE ROOM—slightly larger gold leaf on the door—would be equipped with furnace, hot water heater, fuse box, and, at the starboard end, a sea green Bendix Deluxe laundry auto-washer machine. At the port side end, there would be an empty space that could be used for storage.

⚓　　⚓　　⚓

Construction on the houses finally began in April, and were ready by Labor Day weekend.

In Cobble Hill, Ilsa, elbows on window ledge, watched one of the men in the dark green overalls emerge from the Dean Street door with another box of her belongings, which he then walked up the ramp leading into the big green and yellow Mayflower truck parked next to the building— Heinrich naturally drawn to this moving company through his admiration of Captain Christopher Jones II, who transported the unhappy Pilgrims across the Atlantic from the horrors of England to beautiful Plymouth Rock.

This was the Saturday morning of Labor Day weekend, 1948, Ilsa and *Mor* not having been aware until twelve hours earlier that they would be shipping out, *Far* informing them during a surprise crew assembly after they had returned home from greeting him at the pier —

"We will be moving from Brooklyn to the village of Lynbrook in Nassau County, Long Island," he said. "We will soon be living the American dream in a modern ship-house equipped with state-of-the-art technology."

Earlier, *Far* had been down on the sidewalk directing the movers, but Ilsa hadn't seen him for about twenty minutes or so until he finally emerged from the building with the Krög girl holding her five-month-old daughter and a weathered suitcase —

"Wait at the curb," *Far* ordered her, then stuck his fingers in his mouth and whistled so loud that it scared the crows off a rooftop ledge across the street. Seconds later, a taxicab pulled up and *Far* started talking to the driver, while mother and child looked up and frowned at the girl watching from the window above. After they got in and the cab had driven away, Ilsa went back to the couch to tell *Mor* about it, but found her in one of her spells where she would stare straight ahead and not respond, which had been happening more often lately, Ilsa knowing she would have to wait for her to come back before telling her.

When the movers had finished loading the truck, Heinrich ordered Wife and girl-child to report downstairs and stand at attention next to the Volvo, while he remained behind to make the final inspection. After looking in each room and closet and finding only an unopened bottle of *Whesskey* in the kitchen cabinet, he was about to disembark when, out of the corner of his eye, he spotted the little misshapen fold in the curtain he had often noticed during physical inspections, but had uncharacteristically never adjusted back to its proper position. This time he did, and, afterwards, he was satisfied that the place was in the same ship-shape condition as the day they arrived.

Down in the butcher shop, seated on a stool behind the counter, looking considerably older than his age, Axel Krög sat waiting to die. After disowning his daughter, whom he had always considered his wife's child anyway, he was now utterly alone in the world. His customer base was gone, the younger generation not having an appetite for reindeer meat and preferring to shop at these new "supermarkets" that were popping up all over, and even the oldtimers felt the place had become too gloomy, the butcher no longer smiling or telling wild tales of cutting in the old country, the passion gone—

With a spring in his pivot, Heinrich emerged from the old building for the last time, saluted it, then opened the passenger side door of the Volvo. He pushed down the seat to allow his daughter to climb into the back, then, after returning it upright, extended his hand for Wife to board—

It had been five years since Ingrid last rode in the Volvo, yet, as soon as the door was closed, she immediately felt sick from that same smell. She managed to hold it down as the PV444 roared through Cobble Hill and up the entrance ramp of the Gowanus Parkway, but, rounding the bend where the Gowanus becomes the Belt, she nearly lost it, and nearly lost it again during the stretch from Coney Island to Marine Park, which reeked so strongly of rotting landfill that even the tightly rolled up windows couldn't keep it from adding to the already sickening smell inside the car. Ultimately, though, it was the roller coaster hill near Valley Stream State Park, across the border in Nassau County where the Belt becomes the Southern State, that finally got her, the long gradual incline followed by a quick rise at the peak and a sudden, steep descent that Heinrich was already familiar with and knew exactly when to accelerate to achieve maximum g-force. Towards the bottom, she cried that she was going to be sick, and, like that fateful night in *Sverige*, Heinrich pulled over and she became seasick all over the shoulder—

Despite his eagerness, Heinrich waited patiently until she finally sat back upright and shut the door—

"Are you finished soiling the Moses road, Wife?" he asked.

"Yes, Heinrich."

"For causing this delay, there will be ten spankings prior to this evening's physical inspection."

"Yes, Heinrich."

"What's a physical inspection, *Far*?" Ilsa asked from the back seat, already knowing what it was from having witnessed it so many times—

"Silence, girl-child!" he roared.

Six minutes later, Heinrich docked the Volvo next to the curb in front of their new home on Hendrickson Avenue, where the Mayflower truck was already backed into the driveway. With *Whesskey* bottle in hand, he disembarked and pivoted around the vehicle, stopping on the sidewalk for a moment to admire his new ship-house and salute the American flag hanging motionless atop the pole. He then noticed Wife and child still sitting in the car—

"Wife! Child! Disembark!" he ordered.

Ingrid, present but still green, emerged from the vehicle, then pulled down the seat for Ilsa, who was in a daze staring at the embarrassingly tasteless structure before them—

Heinrich called them to attention and they saluted the house. He then led them up the driveway and across the backyard patio, stopping just before the back steps —

"This will be the door you will use for boarding and disembarking," he said.

In the Galley, a buzzing, circular, fluorescent tube light on the ceiling provided a harsh white light reflecting sharply off the chrome arm of an electronic device mounted on the wall next to the door —

"This is an electric can opener," he said. "It will greatly simplify the task of opening canned rations. However, only I may operate this device, so, if you have a sealed receptacle in need of opening, you must issue a request and I will open it at the first available opportunity."

He pressed the chrome arm down onto the little black button, setting into motion the earsplitting motor that he revved several times, unaware it was causing Ingrid to black out. After he finally released the arm, the motor slowed, but it never came to a full stop, groaning slower and lower for several minutes like the end of an air raid siren —

That evening, while Ingrid was putting Ilsa to bed, Heinrich, on the fescue-seeded dust of his new backyard, freshly lit Pall Mall in one hand and *Whesskey* tumbler in the other, was watching the red neon of the DAN'S FOODS sign blink against the darkening sky when he started hearing moans similar to those he'd heard near the coordinates —

After leaving Ilsa's quarters, Ingrid, per Heinrich's orders given earlier, proceeded to the Crew Lounge and disrobed, then stood at attention saluting the painting. She remained so for nearly an hour, when she finally heard the Galley door open, then the roar of the electric can opener. Moments later, Heinrich entered the room and removed his civilian attire, which he folded neatly and placed on top of the television set.

Arms akimbo, thing erect, he stood beside her looking at the painting—

"It is a handsome artwork," he said.

"Yes, Heinrich."

"Assume the position."

She bent over the front of the loveseat, hands leaning on the wood-framed backrest, eyes level with the lower portion of the canvas, where the USS *Flatbush* was pushing through the raging Atlantic—

"One," she heard Heinrich say just as his open hand stung her bare bottom, prompting a blackout that lasted several minutes. Upon awakening, she found herself nude and seated upright on the loveseat, the cushion wet beneath her tender bottom, while, outside, the Volvo engine fired and roared away—

Heinrich returned two days later, already wearing his Captain's Whites and providing no explanation for his absence. He led them out of the ship-house and on foot to the village rail station nearly a mile away, where, inside the ticket office, he purchased a one-way to Brooklyn for himself and a round-trip for Ingrid—Ilsa was young enough to ride free— and snatched several full-sized, orange-print Long Beach branch timetables, as well as a few of the smaller pocket editions that had the schedule for the Lynbrook station only, all of which he secured in his Captain's Coat interior pocket.

Up 48 stairs they arrived at the platform, where scents of railroad tar and White Castle hamburgers swirled in the September breeze. They had a panoramic view of Sunrise Highway to the south, and, to the north, of Saperstein Plaza, where taxis awaited fares from disembarking passengers, many of whom would stop in for a drink at the *"World*

Famous" Spotted Toad Tavern across the street, Lynbrook's beloved station dive that had a giant sign above the door featuring a cartoon purple toad with yellow polka-dots snatching a bottle of Schlitz with his long amphibian tongue as a dazed fly swirled about his head—

Heinrich led them to the west end of the station, where the first car of a city-bound train would stop, and aligned himself square to the platform edge, with Ingrid and Ilsa falling in behind him. Several minutes later, a train rounded the bend from Centre Avenue and joined the main southern line, then eased into the station, Captain and familial crew saluting its arrival—

Heinrich sat alone, with Ingrid and Ilsa seated together behind him. While some westbound trains stopped at Valley Stream—part of the Far Rockaway branch with the brown timetables—this one did not, though it did stop at St. Albans—part of the West Hempstead branch with the royal blue timetables—where, next to the station, was the giant campus of the St. Albans Naval Hospital, mostly empty now with the War over, but still occupied by those who would never leave alive. Nobody boarded or disembarked here, and, through the open door, a slight breeze came in, brushing Ingrid's cheek, prompting her to black out until they arrived at Jamaica, where they changed trains and boarded a Brooklyn-bound—

While the departure of the *Flatbush* went without incident, Ilsa had to lead *Mor* by the hand all the way home, where she parked her on the loveseat in the Crew Lounge, then started turning the knobs and dials on the television set until the glass grew bright, positioning the two metal wands on top into a perfect "V"—

The looking glass began to glow and emit a high-frequency monotone that traveled deep into Ingrid's ear canal, awakening her not on the loveseat in the Crew Lounge, rather in the audience of a packed theater, surrounded by people laughing hysterically at the antics of a man on stage wearing a wedding gown and smoking a giant cigar—

"That's my son up there!" exclaimed the old woman seated next to her, pointing at the stage—

"What is happening?" Ingrid asked, but the raucous laughter drowned her out. The audience didn't settle down until there was a message from the sponsor, Texaco Gasoline, which is when the old woman finally noticed her—

"Are you okay, cupcake?" she asked.

"I do not know," Ingrid said. "Where am I? I do not even know how I got here—"

"You're in the *Texaco Star Theater* watching my son Milton entertain America. My name is Sandra, by the way, Sandra Berle. You've never seen his show?"

"I think I recognize his voice from the radio, but I've never seen him perform."

"Yep, he's on the radio too. They call him 'Uncle Miltie'. But, after tonight, they're going to know him as 'Mr. Television'."

Up on stage, the Texaco spot came to an end, and, to the delight of the audience, Mr. Television returned with wedding gown and cigar. Ingrid, though, was distracted by a figure just offstage, a tall, lean, blond-haired man in a lab coat, and she gasped—

"What is it, sweetums?" Sandra asked.

"It is Uwe," Ingrid said.

"Uwe? Who's Uwe?"

"He is my—"

She blacked out before she could finish, waking a short

time later in the Crew Lounge. Ilsa was no longer in the room, and the looking glass was dark, except for a point of light in the middle. Deep in her cochlea, the monotone continued, louder, now, in the silence—

⚓   ⚓   ⚓

On the day before Thanksgiving 1948, with Heinrich scheduled to arrive the next morning, Ingrid and Ilsa were at Dan's Foods loading their shopping cart with the makings of an American feast—pre-cooked sixteen-pound turkey that only had to be reheated, sack of Idaho potatoes, can of Libby's extra-gelatinous cranberry sauce, can of Green Giant *great big tender sweet peas*, "home made" pumpkin pie from the bakery, package of *Wasabröd*, two pound block of Swiss cheese, four sticks of extra-salted butter, carton of Pall Mall, box of Smith Brothers black licorice throat drops. On their way to the cash registers, Ingrid stopped short in front of an eight-foot high cardboard advertisement display for Budweiser Lager Beer "Crowntainers", cone-topped twelve-ounce oil cans with an easy twist-off lid. The ad featured a man in black leisure slacks and shiny red smoking jacket over shirt and tie being served a tray topped with Crowntainer and empty glass by his smiling, frilly-aproned wife-servant, and, in the background, a television set tuned to a leather-helmeted running back stiff-arming a toothless linebacker. The top of the display featured a message from Anheuser-Busch: *BUDWEISER LAGER BEER AND TELEVISED FOOTBALL, THE NEW AMERICAN THANKSGIVING TRADITION!*

Ingrid's old *Sex-Tio* instincts kicked in—she always had a knack for knowing what customers wanted, and thought Heinrich would appreciate German beer in an oil can—so she picked up one of the boxed six-packs and placed it in the cart, when Ilsa suddenly exclaimed, "*Mor! Mor! Mor!*"

"What is it, my love?"

"There's a baby in your tummy! No, wait—there's *two* babies in there!"

"How do you know?"

"I can see their shapes moving around!"

Since Labor Day weekend, there had been numerous physical inspections during Heinrich's homecomings, which were usually every three or four weeks. One of them hit the mark, then, days later, a zygotic split occurred at the exact moment of a cosmic disruption detected by the Hooker Telescope on Mount Wilson, noted in that night's log by Edwin Hubble, *"11:16 pm: a blip near Boötes, nothing unusual"*—

Ingrid, lightheaded, knew a blackout was imminent, and that she needed to get back to the looking glass—

"Let us go, my love," she said to Ilsa. "And do not say anything about this to *Far*. I will tell him myself during our Thanksgiving feast."

Early the next morning, Ingrid and Ilsa set out in the cold to greet *Far* at the pier in Brooklyn, a routine already well-familiar to Ilsa, who had a natural instinct for the workings of mass transportation. This time, though, they greeted him considerably earlier than usual—the *Flatbush* normally docked at 4:00 pm and they would get back to the house at around 7:00, then they would eat their rib-eyes ten minutes later—so, when they got back to the house, Ilsa knew they would have to keep *Far* occupied for several hours before their Thanksgiving feast was ready, and offered to have *Mor* fix a plate of *Wasabröd* spread with butter and topped with sliced Swiss cheese, and a Budweiser Crowntainer—

"What is this 'Crowntainer' you speak of, girl-child?" he

asked.

"It's part of the new American Tradition, *Far*," Ilsa said. "Budweiser is the lager beer you're supposed to drink while watching televised football. Then, when it's over, you sup on turkey and pumpkin pie."

"Where are these Crowntainers?"

"In the fridge. Shall I have one brought into the Crew Lounge?"

"Yes. And the *Wasabröd*. Dismissed."

Heinrich had not yet taken opportunity to use the television set, but, with his familiarity of radio equipment, he instinctively knew how to power it on, turn the station selector knob, and adjust the antenna sticks until the static cleared and a grayscale image appeared of men chasing each other across a field daubed with white chalk lines. Through the vibrating speaker, a smooth baritone provided the narrative— *"This has been quite a battle on the gridiron here at Tiger Stadium between the Chicago Cardinals and the Detroit Lions… Now would be the perfect time to remind our viewers that this live national television broadcast is being brought to you by the good folks at Chesterfield cigarettes, the tobacco brand recommended by four out of five doctors…"*

Moments later, Ingrid came in with a tray of butter-and-Swiss covered *Wasabröd*, a delidded Crowntainer, and an empty drinking glass, all of which she placed on the little square table in front of the loveseat—

"Will there be anything else, Heinrich?" she asked.

"No. I will inform you if I need something. Otherwise, do not disturb me while I am viewing this gridiron football match. Dismissed."

After Wife had gone back to the Galley, Heinrich, crunching *Wasabröd* and sipping straight from the

Crowntainer, was soon absorbed in the action from Detroit, impressed with the mettle of these muddy soldiers skirmishing on the gridiron battlefield—

"This football is vonderful," he said out loud to himself, then, looking at the Crowntainer, "As is this Budveiser. The *Deutsch* know their lager."

Minutes later, he was shouting at the television, spewing utterances such as "Oomph!", "Boom!", and "Whap!" whenever the man with the ball was brought down to the slop and piled upon. He had no rooting interest in the contest, which was for the better, as it was nearly impossible to tell the teams apart with the players' uniforms covered with mud on the colorless set.

Shortly after the game ended—the Cardinals besting the Lions, 28-14—Heinrich heard the tingle of the Tiffany sterling silver dinner bell, a housewarming gift from Father-Dr. Panini—

In the Galley, Ilsa, furious, exclaimed, "How dare you, *Mor*! I was supposed to ring the dinner bell, not you!"

Heinrich, rising from the loveseat, froze when he heard the bell ring a second time—

"What is this second bell?" he called out, then proceeded to the Galley—

Ilsa stopped ringing when *Far* came in—

"Who authorized this signal change?" he roared.

"I apologize, Heinrich," Ingrid said. "I had promised Ilsa she could ring the bell, but I had forgotten and rang it myself, so I allowed her to do it—"

"That will be ten spankings. Only you, Wife, as appointed Galley Maid, are permitted to ring the dinner bell one time when the meal is ready for consumption. Is this understood?"

"Yes, Heinrich."

"*Far,*" said Ilsa, smirking, holding a can of cranberry sauce in one hand and a can of peas in the other, "I officially request the delidding of these cans."

Heinrich retrieved the receptacles from her and delidded them perfectly with the electric can opener, causing Ingrid to black out until the motor wound down—

The Captain's Table was set with additional housewarming gifts from Father-Dr. Panini, per written request of Ilsa—burgundy Le Jacquard Français damask tablecloth, Spode North American Harvest Collection dinner plates, Libbey Rock Sharpe Normandy-style wine glasses, sterling Tiffany silverware with matching candlestick holders, Waterford Crystal ashtrays—all of which made the reheated turkey, the cranberry gelatin, the baked potatoes, and the pumpkin pie appear as if they had been prepared in the kitchen of American royalty—

After all were seated, Heinrich tapped stemware with fork and ordered all to bow their heads—

"On this day," he said, "we give thanks to the great Transport Captain, Christopher Jones, Junior, the Second, who navigated the *Mayflower* across the Atlantic to Plymouth Rock, where the Pilgrims commenced this great American holiday, even before America itself had commenced. Now, let us feast."

He tore a drumstick from the turkey, dousing it with triple-iodized salt from the Waterford shaker, then bit off a hunk. Except for his nasal-hair-breathing-grunt-chewing, and the tingle of sterling upon Spode, the meal was eaten in silence.

Ten minutes later, Heinrich began dabbing his lips with his napkin, which Ingrid knew to mean that he was finished eating, and it was now permissible to speak—

"Was the meal satisfactory, Heinrich?"

"Yes, Wife," he said, lighting a Pall Mall, tossing the expired matchstick into the ashtray.

"I am happy to hear this, Heinrich. And now I have some wonderful news to tell you."

"And what is this vonderful news, Wife?"

"Heinrich, I am with child—"

"She's with two childs, *Far*!" Ilsa exclaimed.

"What is the girl-child saying?"

"She thinks there are two children in my belly, but we have no proof of this. Only God would know such a thing."

"And what does Father-Dr. Panini have to say about this?"

"I have not spoken to Father-Dr. Panini as of yet."

"Then how do you know you are with child?"

"Ilsa saw the shape of the child in my belly at Dan's Foods."

"You could see the child?" Heinrich asked Ilsa.

"I could see *both* childs, *Far*," she smirked.

Heinrich slammed the table with his palm, causing the silverware to jump. He then rose abruptly, knocking backwards his Captain's Dining Chair—

"Damn it, Wife!" he roared. "There had better be only one child in there, a masculine child! This is an order!"

⚓   ⚓   ⚓

It was hot out there, but even hotter inside, when one of them made a break for it and burst the sac. They were the exact same age—at one point they had been the same being—but one was clearly dominant and destined to be the first one out, and, ultimately, the Heir, while the other would forever be his underling, who, in the wake of his brother's flight, was being repeatedly kicked in the head.

Eventually, the kicking stopped, which is when the underling finally realized it had been abandoned, and started kicking his own legs until his brother's feet were once more pounding his head. Then the cave walls started shaking, followed by a great pucker, and suddenly his brother was gone, leaving him alone in this reeking, noisy place, a horror compared to the gentle bubbles of the amniotic sea. The walls started shaking again, gently at first, but growing stronger, until he was thrust upward in a great queef. A short time later it happened again, and, despite the path having already been widened, his crown got caught on the way out. The next one, though, would surface him into a world of painful light, and his brother's angry cries—

Independence Day, 1949, not even noon and it was already 90° with a soupy humidity making it feel like over 100.

Ilsa, on the Crew Lounge floor, surrounded by crusty Bloomingdale's catalogs, sensing that something was about to happen, looked back at *Mor* on the loveseat, her belly so large that she could only sit partially upright with her head leaning against the backrest and tilted forward just enough to see the looking glass tuned to an encore presentation of *The Howdy Doody Show*, her face expressionless, the only glimmer in her eye the reflection of the dull glow across the room—

The air conditioning was broken inside NBC Studio 3A at Rockefeller Center, where Ingrid was beached in the front row of a small set of bleachers full of girls and boys dressed in stringed cowboy hats and leather chaps giving wide berth to the sweaty fat lady, putting those seated at the edges precariously close to going over. Up on stage, Buffalo Bob, with a puppet in each hand—one of them Howdy Doody, *the rootenist tootenist red-headedest 48-freckled puppet in the land*, and the other a blond-haired doll clad in lab coat holding a mouth mirror and sickle probe—was doing a live read for *"the really big 3 Musketeers milk chocolate and fluffy nougat candy bar"*, when Clarabell the Clown, played by Lynbrook-born Bob Keeshan, broke character and said, "Hey, uh, Bob, I think there's something wrong with that lady over there in the Peanut Gallery—"

Ingrid, about to cry for help, felt something drop from her nether region, a pink, reeking fluid that splattered on the scuffed linoleum beneath her. The children around her started screaming and jumping off the bleachers, nearly causing a stampede at the exits—

"Mor! Mor! Mor!" Ilsa exclaimed.

Suddenly back in the Crew Lounge, Ingrid tried to focus on Ilsa pointing at the pink splatter on the floor and on her Bloomingdale's catalogs—

"What has happened, my love?" she asked, then blacked out again, prompting Ilsa to hurry out of the room and dial the hospital—

On Woodland Drive in Rockville Centre, Father-Dr. Carmine Panini, seated at his kitchen table, sipping coffee from a *TIJ Hospital* mug, a freshly lit Benson & Hedges burning in a *TIJ* ashtray, was daydreaming about the annual Fourth of July block party on Christopher Street that would commence in a few short hours, and reminiscing about last year's party—during which several men in tight leather short-pants and studded motorcycle caps unscrewed the fire hydrants with giant wrenches and everyone started dancing—when the telephone rang down the hall, prompting a heavenward roll of the eyes—

"Ingrid von Schatt just broke her water and her husband is away at sea," reported Sister Golden Hair on the other end.

After another eye-roll, the Father-Dr. said he would have a cab sent to bring her and her daughter to the hospital, then, before hanging up, added, "Let Sister Enid handle this one." He knew he would need his toughest soldier for this delivery, and there were no tougher maternity nurses than Sister Enid Stern, a descendant of the Gulches of North Platte, Nebraska. For the past several months, he had been driving over to Lynbrook to check on Mrs. von Schatt, and it turned out that Ilsa had been correct—there were definitely two in there, which was now easy to tell with all the elbows and feet poking at her belly—yet, their combined presence, which should have been radiating like a binary star system, had only a single faint glow, his concern reaching the point that he discreetly brought his personal exorcism kit to the hospital and kept it in his office closet, just in case—

Scrubbed and bespectacled in her iron-forged rims, Sister Enid entered Delivery Room #6, where Mrs. Heinrich von Schatt had just been wheeled in and buckled to the stirrup chair. The sister-nurse ordered everyone out, including the girl she had delivered nearly five years earlier.

"Are you in pain?" she asked Mrs. von Schatt after everyone had gone, but the patient was looking past her and did not respond.

"Okey-dokey, then," said the sister-nurse. "Makes my job easier."

Seasoned as she was, she had never before seen a soul as dark as the first of the von Schatt twins she would deliver, a male. Six minutes later came the brother, this one at least having a faint glow, like a dying Lampyridae.

After the newborns had been placed in the warmers, Sister Enid summoned Sister Golden Hair to take over, then proceeded to Father-Dr. Panini's office—

"Completely dark?" he asked, feigning surprise, lighting a Benson & Hedges. "Like *The Raven?*"

"Darker."

"Like *The Batman?*"

"Try *Satan*, Father."

"*Il Diavolo, Mamma Mia!* What about the other?"

"Low wattage. But at least the Heavenly Father is giving that one a chance, slim as it may be."

After being kicked out of the delivery room, Ilsa went straight to Father-Dr. Panini's office and borrowed his telephone to call the newly-promoted Rear Admiral Upper Half Arnold Houlihan at the Bush Terminal so he could inform *Far* why they were not there to greet him, and that, upon arrival, he should proceed directly to The Infant Jesus Hospital—

"I'll have a Captain's Special Transport Vehicle waiting at the pier to bring him directly there," said the Rear Admiral Upper Half.

"Thank you, *darling*."

Late the following afternoon, Father-Doctor Panini, seated behind his desk at TIJ, sipping coffee doused generously with Sambuca, a Benson & Hedges burning in the ashtray, still hungover—the births of the von Schatt twins yesterday had been quick enough for him to make it to the Village in time for the unscrewing of the fire hydrants—was only now beginning to contemplate the potential horrors that God had unleashed upon humanity with these foggy souls, when the son of the Devil himself, erect and clad in crisp, painfully bright Captain's Whites, pivoted into the office and saluted—

"I am here to claim my Male Heir," he announced.

"Captain von Schatt, it is very nice to see you—and, congratulations!"

"Where is my Heir, Father?"

"Please come with me," the Father-Doctor said, rising from his chair, stamping out his cigarette. "I am sure you will be very pleased by what I have to show you."

Unaware of everything that had happened since her water broke the day before, Ingrid's subconscious, sensing Heinrich's presence, awakened her. She found herself looking at fluorescent tube lighting on the ceiling, and feeling a strange sensation on her chest. There was also an odd sucking sound nearby, and she lifted her head just enough to see a newborn attached to each of her nipples, prompting her to scream—

Out in the corridor, Father-Dr. Panini and Captain von Schatt heard the scream and hurried into the room—

Seeing Heinrich burst in, Ingrid attempted to get up and salute, but her body did not respond—

"Mrs. von Schatt, what is the matter?" the Father-Dr. asked.

She tried to speak, but could not—

"I have consumed no *Whesskey*, yet I am seeing double," Heinrich said.

"Congratulations times two, Captain von Schatt!" said the Father-Doctor with as much cheer as he could muster, a sorry effort compared to the cheering he'd been doing 24 hours earlier when they broke out the wrenches on Christopher Street—

"Father, is this some sort of parlor trick?"

"No, Captain von Schatt. This is no trick, I assure you. These are your beautiful twin sons, delivered directly from the... Hand of God, yes, the Hand of God. Oh, forgive me, Father—"

"Wife!" Heinrich roared, startling the Father-Dr., as well as

Sister Golden Hair passing in the corridor. "I explicitly ordered you to produce *one* Male Heir!"

When Mother blacked out again, the twins stopped sucking their beestings and looked up at the blazing blue eyes—

"What will you name them, Captain von Schatt?" the Father-Doctor asked.

"They shall be named Heinrich II and Heinrich III, after their father. Whichever one came out first shall be Heinrich II, the First Male Heir."

The Captain saluted the Father, the sons, and the blacked out Wife, then pivoted out of the room, to the CSTV waiting for him in front of the hospital's main entrance. He instructed the driver to drop him off at the Lynbrook ship-house, where, after a stop in the Galley for a block of Swiss cheese and two Budweiser Crowntainers, he jumped in the Volvo and roared towards the blazing sunset, and Valley Stream—

Ilsa, having spent the night in the smoke-filled waiting room under the supervision of Sister Betty Veronica, who had initially been ordered by Sister Enid to keep the girl away from her baby brothers, was finally brought in to meet them after the Captain had departed—

"What are their names?" she asked Father-Dr. Panini.

"Well, I was just about to go over that with your *Mamma*. Captain von Schatt said they shall both be named Heinrich, and the older one shall be First Male Heir—"

"Oh, please, *darling*," she said, rolling her eyes. "*First Male Heir*—What about First *Female* Heir?"

Turning to Ingrid, who was fading in and out, the Father-Dr. said, "If I may, Mrs. von Schatt, I have a thought. For the sake of your boys, to avoid the confusion of being identical twins with the same name, why don't you give them different first names, and use 'Heinrich' as their middle names. This way, it will be, let us say, 'Joseph Heinrich II von Schatt' and 'Peter Heinrich III von Schatt', so you will still be abiding by your husband's wishes to name them 'Heinrich', yet sparing them future confusion about their individual identities."

Ingrid did not respond, so he turned back to the girl—

"That's fine, *darling*," she said, "but 'Joseph' and 'Peter' are dreadful. Let's instead go with 'Walter' and 'Herman'."

"Like the jewelry counter clerks at Bloomingdale's?"

"You know them, *darling*?"

"I have made their acquaintance on several occasions. Is 'Walter' and 'Herman' acceptable to you, Mrs. von Schatt?"

"Yes, Heinrich," Ingrid said weakly.

⚓   ⚓   ⚓

This was going to be the score that would finally earn Parnell the kind of respect that most black men usually didn't get in the white man's world, especially from an outfit like the Panini Family, who had entrusted him with the midnight hijacking of a tractor-trailer on Conduit Boulevard coming from Idlewild Airport loaded with pallets of totally, totally untraceable U.S. currency used by American servicemen stationed overseas.

Pulling the truck over was easy—the driver just gave it up, and Parnell gave the guy a few bucks to catch a cab home. Up to this point, everything had gone smoothly, but then he got lazy and didn't bother opening the trailer doors to check the load—which, if he had, he would have still had a chance to let this wrong truck loaded with thousands of sea green cans of Similac baby formula continue on, and hijack the correct truck with the cash in it—a fuckup that would earn

Parnell a bullet in the head from the gun of none other than Jimmy "Da Meanie" Panini himself.

⚓   ⚓   ⚓

Satiated, Herman stopped sucking Mother's teat and belched. Once more he looked up, hoping this time she would notice him, but, as usual, she was oblivious. He started kicking at her, but instead struck Walter in the leg, who responded with a swift, precise return kick. The underling started to cry, which only further annoyed the Heir, who kicked him even harder, making the underling wail even louder —

In the autumn, Ilsa started kindergarten, while Ingrid spent most of her days and evenings on the loveseat in the Crew Lounge, television on, a twin attached to each bruised and swollen nipple. Then, around Columbus Day, the well ran dry, and Father-Dr. Panini had 6,000 cans of Similac baby formula delivered by his eleventh and thirteenth cousins Sal and Carmine, who nearly killed themselves on the narrow Lower Deck stairs bringing them down to the Engine Room hold, until they "borrowed" a roller conveyer from Dan's Foods.

Ilsa, recognizing the decline in *Mor*'s ability to care for the twins and perform routine household chores, neither of which she was about to start helping with beyond the handling of *Mor*'s allowance from *Far* prior to each departure, noticed a post on the bulletin board inside the entrance to Dan's Foods advertising *"CHEAP CHEAP DOMESTIC HELP, ALL HOUSEHOLD CHORES AND CHILDCARE DUTIES"*, which she would soon learn was posted by Lang Tang, owner of The Best Great Wall Chinese Food Restaurant Takeout Laundry, whose twelve-year-old daughter, Thang, was available for work at shockingly low rates. She hired Thang to come over six times daily at a dollar a day to feed the twins and change their cloth diapers—the boys would not enjoy the disposable silk their sister had, their messes contained in regular old cotton that had to be laundered—which Thang would take to the restaurant each evening and bring back clean in the morning.

Each can of Similac contained a full pound of formula, of which one "normal sized" infant would consume two-three ounces every four hours, totaling one can per day. The von Schatt twins, at first, split an entire can at each feeding, then, over their first winter, rode the pig, each finishing a full can every four hours. The electric can opener received heavy use by Thang, except during the brief occasions when Heinrich was home, when Ilsa had to request him open them. By spring, the boys had become giant toddlers, and, without any toys to play with, they thump-crawled all over the house destroying everything they encountered.

On a summer's morn not long before the twins' first birthday, Ingrid was seated in the *Howdy Doody* Peanut Gallery looking around for Uwe when Ilsa burst into the studio shouting, "*Mor! Mor! Mor!* Walter's trying to walk!"

Tired of being on the floor, Walter took an awkward step forward before swiftly falling at Mother's feet. Angry, he bit her ankle with his sharp little teeth, and she screamed. Then, using the front of the loveseat frame to pull himself back up, he turned and took two quick steps towards his sister before falling again. But he got right back up, and this time made it to Ilsa, then back to the loveseat, where he grabbed Mother's forearm and took another bite, and she screamed again—

Herman, meanwhile, disinterested in his brother's exploits, stared at the television. It would be several more weeks before he would attempt upright navigation, but he too would be walking by their first birthday, which Ilsa decided to celebrate by taking Ingrid and the twins to the playground.

There was a sandbox, monkey bars, swings, and several benches with layers of flaking green lead paint, only one of which was situated in the shade. On any other sunny day, the place would have been full of children and mothers, but, today, the Fourth of July, they had it to themselves, as most of the other families in the village were packing coolers and charcoal into their cars getting ready to head out to Jones Beach or Salisbury Park or some other such place where they would remain until nightfall to watch patriotic Chinese fireworks for ten minutes, then all leave at the same time and cause a massive late-night traffic jam on the parkways. For the hour they were there, Herman remained in the sandbox building small mounds with what little sand there was, while Walter investigated the playground perimeter picking up small objects—beer can pull-tabs, discarded cigarette butts, liquor bottle shards, a fingertip. Ingrid, meanwhile, seated on the shaded bench, drifted in and out, as Ilsa, next to her, flipped through her catalogs.

During that summer of 1950, the playground became part of the daily routine for Walter and Herman, but not for Ingrid and Ilsa after Thang took over the chore for an extra 50 cents a day and an additional quarter per diem to buy the boys a "treat" from The Stationery Store. Herman would pick out a pack of Viceroy candy cigarettes, while Walter, despite having no interest in baseball or trading cards, would pick out a pack of America Leaf Tobacco Company baseball cards and give them to Herman, but keep for himself the little pouch of tobacco that came with each pack and suck on it between feedings. Thang would pick out a pack of Parliament cigarettes for herself, smoking them while sitting on the playground bench watching the boys through her counterfeit Ray-Bans, taking tiny drags, exhaling like a movie star, ashing more than necessary. Herman played alone in the sandbox, digging with the rust-flaked backhoe bolted into the concrete beneath what was left of the sand, while Walter, scowling, patrolled the playground perimeter, watching the other children, confronting them if he saw them doing something suspicious, or if they just didn't look right, and especially if they got too close to Herman.

On a sweltering morning in August, the playground crowded, Walter, from a distance, watched Herman in the sandbox reach for a bright yellow cast-iron Tonka dump truck that had been momentarily abandoned by a boy with wild, curly black hair—

After being slapped by his mustachioed grandmother for wetting his short pants, Gregos spied the kid in the sandbox playing with his Tonka and stormed over—

"Don't touch my truck!" he yelled, but the kid in the diaper and stained undershirt ignored him, continuing to push the toy around and make engine noises. Gregos then grabbed the front end of it and tried to yank it away, but the kid held on to the back end with surprising strength and wouldn't let go—

Already approaching, Walter stepped over the sandbox frame and shoved the curly-haired boy, who lost his grip on the truck and fell backwards, the back of his head hitting the thin layer of sand over concrete—

Gregos, with thirteen older siblings and no stranger to being pushed around, jumped to his feet ready to start swinging until he noticed the look in the toddler's eye—

"Giagiá!" he cried, stumbling over the sandbox frame as

he ran back to the benches. *"Giagiá, o diávolos, Giagiá!"*

Giagiá was about to give him another slap until she caught a glimpse of the boy in the sandbox and saw that her *engonós* was not fibbing—

"Páme, Gregos," she said gravely, whisking the boy under her shawl and short-stepping him away towards the Avenue—

⚓   ⚓   ⚓

Ilsa knew that, as soon as *Far* noticed the twins walking, the trips to the pier to greet and send off the *Flatbush* would resume, a requirement suspended when they were born, pending upright ambulation. She was able to successfully hide it for six months whenever *Far* was home for his brief layovers, luring them into her quarters with baseball cards for Herman and tobacco pouches for Walter, with the promise of more if they stayed in the room and kept quiet until they heard *Far's* car drive away. She knew, though, that this was not sustainable, and, with *Mor* drifting further away each day, she would have to train them herself.

In the days leading to Christmas 1950, she ran her brothers through the old drills that *Mor* had run with her five years earlier, which she still remembered perfectly. Every morning at the crack of dawn, before the start of the broadcast day when the channels were still airing test patterns, and before *Mor* had begun her daylong occupation of the loveseat, the children would assemble in the Crew Lounge and practice falling into line, standing at attention, and saluting *Far's* painting—

Heinrich would finally notice during Christmas dinner, seated at the head of the Captain's Table with Wife and girl-child before him, while the Male Heirs dined in the Galley, tied at the waist in their already outgrown highchairs with sections of nautical rope that their sister had found in the garage workshop while snooping for valuables, secured behind the chairs by skillfully tied constrictor knots learned from a book she happed upon in the West End Elementary School library titled *All You'll Ever Need to Know About Knots and Boys*, which, despite the cover photograph depicting three lassoed Cub Scouts with unbuttoned navy blue uniform shirts and yellow wolfkerchiefs around their necks, was not a sanctioned publication of the Boy Scouts of America. Earlier, Walter became angry when Ilsa tied him into the chair, and even angrier after he had finished his meatballs and wanted to get out. After failing to find a way to free himself, the boy's keen eye caught the glint of chrome, and he started throwing his weight towards the device on the wall, managing to scooch the highchair across the faux brick vinyl composite flooring a couple of inches at a time, while his brother, oblivious, continued gorging on mashed potatoes and lingonberries with his hands, blobs of magenta mush all over face, tray, and floor—

At the Captain's Table, freshly lit Pall Mall burning in the ashtray next to his Spode Christmas tree plate, Heinrich had just taken another bite of his ribeye when he heard the motor in the Galley—

"Who dares operate my electric can opener?" he roared, slamming silverware on Spode, rising swiftly, knocking the chair backwards, pivoting through the swinging door into the Galley—

Despite his young age, Walter understood the gravity of his defiance, and again pressed the chrome arm down just as the swinging door flew open and Father burst in—

Heinrich, after a long day of *Whesskey* and Crowntainers that began early with the opening of presents—five individually addressed envelopes sent by post from The Infant Jesus Hospital, each containing a Christmas card from "Santa" stuffed with five untraceable twenty dollar bills and a gift certificate good for one free meal at Mama Panini's Italian Restaurant on Mulberry Street—was still seeing double, so he used Hosenpinkel's old trick of squint-blinking five times fast and waiting for one of them to come into focus, which, in this case, turned out to be the one on the left, furthest from the can opener—

"Heinrich! That will be fifty spankings!"

Unaware that their middle names were "Heinrich", or that they even had middle names, Walter looked at Herman working the mashed potatoes, then back at Father, whose blazing blue eyes were now locked on the underling—

Not realizing his son was tied down, Heinrich attempted to lift him out of the highchair, but lifted both boy and chair. He tried shaking him out, but eventually lost his grip. The chair dropped to the vinyl composite and made a wood-cracking sound upon impact. For a moment, boy and chair remained upright, before slowly leaning over and eventually crashing down on its side in front of the Philco—

"Wife!" Heinrich roared, as the potato-lathered boy began to scream. "Remove this Heir from his chair at once!"

Ingrid, hearing her husband's roar, hurried into the Galley, followed by Ilsa, who knew that *Mor* would never be able to untie the constrictor knots—

After Herman had been untied by his sister, Ingrid lifted the screaming boy from the wreckage. She placed him on the floor, but he promptly pushed himself up and dashed into the Crew Lounge—

"Wow, Herman's first steps!" Ilsa exclaimed.

"Wife, why have I not been informed that this child can ambulate?"

"We didn't know either, *Far*," Ilsa said.

"Silence, girl-child! Wife, retrieve the AWOL Heir for his discipline!"

Ingrid retrieved her youngest son from the Crew Lounge, setting off another round of screaming and a fresh deposit in the boy's diaper, on top of the hardened load he'd already been sitting on. She handed him to Heinrich, now seated in one of the *Plasticizer 6000* chairs, waiting to place the insubordinate boy over his knee—

"Wife!" he roared after discovering the reeking mess in the diaper. "Clean this child immediately so I can discipline him proper!"

Ingrid scrubbed the boy's bottom clean in the Galley sink, while Ilsa untied Walter and stashed him in her quarters with a fresh tobacco pouch. Naked and screaming, Herman was handed back to Heinrich, who positioned him over his knee and addressed his bare bottom with two practice strokes before striking for real, counting after each, the child's cries so intense that, by the mid-twenties, they were inaudible to human ears.

After the fiftieth spank, Heinrich rose and handed the boy back to Ingrid, then stepped over the fallen highchair to the can opener, pressing down the arm and letting it roar for several seconds before disembarking via the back door—

In Ilsa's quarters, Walter, with juicy tobacco pouch between cheek and gum, heard the Volvo engine ignite and back out of the driveway, then roar off into the silent night—

Heinrich returned three days later, clad in Captain's Whites, ready for departure. In short order, the von Schatts of

Lynbrook set out for the first time as a quintet, into the frigid December air, the village covered with two fresh inches of snow fallen overnight. The twins were bundled in puffy winter coats, hats, mittens, mufflers, and boots that their sister had mail-ordered from Sears, while Ingrid wore an elegant new green dress, coat, and shoes ordered from Abraham & Straus. Ilsa fashioned a red Dior dress from Bloomingdale's and a custom-fitted mink from Fritz the Furrier of Garden City. Heinrich did not wear a coat over his Captain's Whites, which gleamed so bright they made the snow look dirty.

With a twin in each hand, Ingrid did her best to keep pace with her husband while struggling to hold on to both Walter and Herman, the former walking fast and trying to break free of her grip, the latter walking so slow that she had to pull him along every few steps, while Ilsa brought up the rear, rolling her eyes at the slow pace. When they finally made it to the warmth of the station ticket office, their cheeks were pink and their teeth were chattering, except for their Captain, who walked in as if from a spring breeze —

"Be careful up on the platform," the agent warned as he slid the tickets beneath the window bars. "There's some patches of ice up there, so watch where you walk."

Up the 48 steps to the old wood-planked platform warped with dips and valleys in which lingering puddles had frozen, Heinrich led his family to the west end of the station, where the first car of a city-bound train would stop. At the waiting spot, Heinrich stood at the edge of the platform, with Ingrid falling in line behind him, followed by the First Male Heir, the Second Male Heir, and the girl-child.

Minutes later, a train originating from Long Beach rounded the bend from Centre Avenue and slowly pulled into the station. Heinrich saluted the Train Captain seated in his booth, his example followed by Ingrid and the children. After the doors slid open, he stepped over the gap and onto the train, pivoting towards his preferred seat across the aisle from the Train Captain's booth, unaware that Wife was not behind him—

While following Heinrich onto the train, Ingrid slipped on a patch of ice and fell hard on the platform, landing on her right hip. While nothing had broken, the pain was excruciating and she was unable to get up. She called for her husband, but he had already disappeared into the train car, and her voice was being drowned by the prevailing platform winds—

"I'll get *Far!*" Ilsa exclaimed, leaping over *Mor*'s legs, then the gap, not realizing the twins would follow—

Walter confidently stepped over Mother's legs, then the gap, while Herman walked around her and nearly stepped into the void between train and platform—

Finally realizing Wife wasn't with him, Heinrich looked out the window and saw her lying on the platform. He rose and passed his children approaching in the aisle, then disembarked just as the door was sliding shut—

"Wife!" he roared, standing over her on the platform, the winds unable to drown him out. "Rise this instant before you further embarrass me!"

"Heinrich, I cannot get up!" she cried, clutching her injured hip. Then, noticing the train behind him starting to move, she pointed and screamed, "Heinrich! The children! They are on the train!"

"Wife! Rise this instant! This is an order!" he roared, ignoring her cries, taking no notice of the train gliding away behind him—

Palms against glass, Ilsa watched the platform slide away,

prompting a moment of panic, until she recognized the opportunity with which she had just been presented —

Fifteen minutes later, from the east, beyond the Long Beach spur, the shimmering headlamps of a westbound train originating from Babylon appeared down the line. Ingrid knew she had best get to her feet and board this train or else Heinrich would become even angrier, prompting a release of adrenaline that enabled her to push herself up without the help of her husband, who wasn't offering it, and stand at attention, slightly askew, saluting the train as it pulled into the station. After the doors slid open and Heinrich boarded, Ingrid gingerly stepped over the gap and limped to her designated seat behind him, then blacked out —

Walter watched the old brick factories drift by out the window as the train rolled through the industrial wastelands of Queens, where, despite the midday hour, the big red neon sign atop the Swingline staple factory glowed bright against the chimney-smoked sky. As much as he liked the gloom, his favorite part of the ride was the train descending into the tunnel below the East River, when the outside world went black and his ears clogged, and his menacing reflection appeared on the dark window staring back at him. Herman too had been enjoying the ride, particularly the doors sliding open and shut at each station, but he didn't like the tunnel and was unable to pop his clogged ears, which made him cry, causing the clogging to become even worse —

Still disoriented after being abruptly pulled from her blackout, having momentarily forgotten about the children, Ingrid's survival instinct gave her the singular task of keeping pace with Heinrich as they navigated the Atlantic Avenue Terminal to the BMT subway platform, which she managed successfully, until they were seated on the train and she went dark again until 59th Street. She nearly blacked out as they ascended the urine-reeking subway stairwell up to the street and fell behind, but made up ground during the two-block walk to the BAT. It wasn't until they stepped into the beaming winter sunlight of the Building B atrium that she remembered the children, but Ilsa knew how to get to the designated spot, and she and the twins may already be waiting there, she hoped—

But they weren't there. Having pulled ahead, Heinrich stood alone at the spot waiting for her to hobble to him. Finally, she arrived and saluted, and Heinrich saluted back, then, without a word, pivoted away towards the *Flatbush* gangway—

Knowing Heinrich would be preoccupied with official Captain matters for the next couple of hours—enough time, perhaps, to find the children and bring them back before departure at 1600, when Heinrich would be on the Bridge watching for them—Ingrid, after seeing him disappear into the ship, dropped her salute and hobbled back down the pier towards the subway. Fully conscious now, she took the #2 back to Atlantic Avenue and searched the L.I.R.R. platforms and waiting room, but they were nowhere to be seen. It then occurred to her that they may have disembarked at Jamaica, so she took the next train there and searched the platforms and waiting rooms, but again did not find them. At one point she asked a patrolman if he had seen a six-year-old girl with twin one-year-old boys, but all he said was, "Sorry, lady. You married?"

It then occurred to her where Ilsa would go. Abandoning all hope of making it back to the pier in Brooklyn before departure, she boarded the next train to Penn Station—

Ilsa escorted her brothers through the heavy revolving

door. On the other side, like magic, the sparkling white palace opened before them.

"Isn't it amazing?" she asked, then led them to the jewelry counter—

"Our princess has arrived!" exclaimed Herman, the blond-haired jewelry clerk.

"And, with her," added Walter, the other, dark-haired, pencil-mustached, goateed jewelry clerk, and Herman's lover, "two handsome young princes who I'm sure will grow up to be a pair of strapping young men."

"*Darlings*," Ilsa said, "these are my twin brothers, Walter and Herman."

"Oh, precious joy!" Herman exclaimed, clutching his heart, "The princes are named for us!"

"How *divine*," Walter said, he too clutching, looking at his namesake, until he felt a chill at the way the boy was staring back at him—

An hour later, Ingrid arrived at the counter, and Herman the jewelry clerk informed her that the girl was over in makeup—

"Hi, *Mor*!" Ilsa said, sitting in the chair being lipsticked and rouged, the twins nowhere in sight. "Don't I look *divine*?"

"Where are the babies?" Ingrid cried.

"They're up in the International Toy Department, *darling*."

Unbeknownst to Ilsa, they were no longer in the International Toy Department up on the fourth floor, but in the Security Office holding pen down in the basement, brought there after Walter had deliberately broken off all four legs of a female Dala horse in front of a horrified sales clerk. Herman, meanwhile, had been marching around the fourth floor banging a red-and-white metal drum, the contents of his overloaded diaper running down his legs and leaving a trail of brown drops and dribbles on the highly buffed white linoleum store walkways, prompting numerous faints, complaints, and eye rolls from aghast clientele. By the time Ingrid and Ilsa showed up, International Toys was closed for cleaning and sterilizing, and they were directed to a padded service elevator that took them down to the basement, where the boys were released upon payment of Dala horse and drum, Ilsa handling the transaction with cash extracted from her Floricha Cruz iguana skin wallet—

At precisely 1600 hours, Captain Heinrich von Schatt blew the horn signaling the departure of the *USS Flatbush*, then looked one last time at the vacant spot down on Pier 3—

Three weeks later, down in the Male Heirs' Quarters, Walter lie awake, his curiosity astir at the noises above. He slipped out of bed and scaled the steep Lower Deck staircase with natural stealth, one of several strong instincts he'd begun to explore. Through the Galley he proceeded to the port side corridor, then slowly twisted the knob of the Crew Lounge door, opening it just enough to see Mother, naked, bent over the loveseat, and Father, also naked, spanking her bare bottom hard. The boy was surprised she didn't react, until Father later stepped behind her and pushed his thing into her, when she let out a whimper before going silent again. Father grunted as he pushed against her, skin slapping skin, the wooden loveseat frame hitting the wall beneath the painting. This went on for several seconds, ending with Father making a louder, elongated noise, then stepping back from Mother, his big pink thing wet and with strings of fluid dangling from it, the Heir knowing it was time to retreat—

Heinrich looked towards the door, but it was closed, and all was quiet—

⚓   ⚓   ⚓

Seated alone at the Mess Deck Officers' Table, after enduring the bland fish sticks and too-sweet apple juice, the recently appointed First Officer of the *USS Flatbush* bit into his square of cherry crumb cobbler and closed his eyes, savoring what had been the only good thing about being on this old rustbucket, allowing his mouth a moment to savor the tart sweetness before swallowing.

Willis A. Streicher — Alaska native, son of German immigrants who'd fled *Deutschland* during the First War — considered himself a victim of his own success. All he wanted was to go home to Fairbanks, grow his beard back, and start a riverboat dinner cruise business on the Chena — but the Merchant Marine kept promoting him, and the pay grade bumps proved too much to resist.

Then, two weeks ago — early September 1951 — he was appointed First Officer of the *USS Flatbush* with psycho Captain von Schatt, and his life had been a nightmare ever since — except for the cherry crumb cobbler, the one thing he had to look forward to during these long days and nights at sea, which was now being interrupted by an unfolding situation five tables over. Several Airmen were trying to get another Airman to play a song on the acoustic guitar resting on its stand next to the piano in the corner — instruments brought on board by the previous *Flatbush* skipper, Captain Jonas "Sharky" Waters, whose approach to keeping the men in line was to keep them entertained, but had been collecting dust since von Schatt took command.

"This guy can sing and play guitar real good," explained Airman Baker to the others. "I saw him at Lackland. He played a couple of songs every night in the Mess. Everyone loved him!"

"I don't know about everyone," said Airman Cash.

"Come on, man, don't be modest. Just play a song or two."

"Think anyone would mind?"

"No way, man! It'll be swell for morale!"

"Hand me the guitar," said Airman Cash, prompting a cheer that made Streicher nervous—this being a clear disruption of the *Flatbush* "Mess Deck Murmur", of which only the Alcatraz "Mess Hall Din" could compare after Warden "Old Saltwater" Johnston relaxed his famously strict "Code of Silence". Yet, if he tried to put a stop to it, the men might get mad, and then he would have to go tell the Chief Security Officer, whom he was deathly afraid of, and then it would get back to von Schatt, who might yell at him. So he decided to let it play out and hope for the best, while he went into the kitchen and pulled rank to secure another square of cherry crumb cobbler—

Up on the Bridge, Heinrich slowed to 13 knots and picked up his Bausch & Lombs, spying the orange glows on the horizon that, while always in the vicinity of the coordinates, were never in the same place twice. Then the moans started, louder than ever, vibrating the helm knobs, and, once more, he closed his eyes and tried to figure out what they were saying, until his keen ear started picking up something else, causing him to lose focus. It was an old hymn he recognized from somewhere, but not at sea, and he soon realized it was coming not from out there, but from somewhere on the ship. Furious, he blew his bosun's whistle, a signal for all personnel to stop, rise to attention, and remain so until further instruction, and for the First Officer to report immediately to the Bridge—

In the kitchen, about to secure his third cobbler square,

First Officer Streicher heard the whistle and cursed God, then grabbed the square anyway and shoved the whole thing into his mouth at once, swallowing it on his way up to the Bridge—

On the Mess Deck, several thousand servicemen paid no heed to the bosun's whistle, spellbound as they were by the Airman sitting atop one of the tables strumming and crooning a *molto lento* interpretation of "Amazing Grace" with a Southern baritone that was melting their souls. His song revealed to them the gravity of the moment, of leaving behind their families and homeland on a ship transporting them across the dark ocean to the very country where, less than a decade ago, Hitler was still in power. They would then be dispatched to various points in Europe to keep an eye on the Soviets, knowing World War III could break out at any moment, and that it was their turn to defend the free world, just as their fathers, uncles, and grandfathers had done before them. The singing Airman reminded them that they were all in this together for the greater cause, and that all would be fine in the end, whether it be by America saving the world again, or by the mercy of God—

Just outside the Bridge, First Officer Streicher paused to swipe some crumbs off the lapel of his First Officer's Whites, but was unable to remove a dot of magenta cherry stain. He then took a deep breath, straightened his spine, cracked his knuckles, and tapped on the gold-leaf-lettered door window—

"Permission to enter the Bridge, Captain," he said, still in the corridor after opening the door.

"Granted. What is this music on my vessel?"

"There is an Airman with a guitar singing for the men on the Mess Deck, sir."

"And you are permitting this to happen?"

"No, sir. I was about to put a stop to it, then I heard the bosun's whistle and reported here immediately, sir."

"But not before finishing your cherry crumb cobbler?"

"It was already in my mouth, sir. I had to swallow, sir."

"You have an answer for everything, First Officer Streicher. Since you are thus prepared, I will allow you to man the helm while I personally handle the matter down on the Mess Deck. Maintain present course. First Officer on the Bridge. Captain to the Mess."

One of the golden rules on the USS *Flatbush* was for servicemen and crew to rise and salute **IMMEDIATELY** when the Captain appeared on the Mess Deck—which Heinrich seldom did, normally having his meals sent directly to the Bridge. When he did appear, it would take no more than a few seconds for the thousands of dining men to be on their feet, at attention, and saluting in his direction—a task complicated by the picnic-style tables with attached benches on either side that they had to hurriedly climb out of from the seated position.

Tonight, however, when he appeared, not a single serviceman, nor any of the ship's crew, noticed the gleaming Captain's Whites in the doorway, so moved were they by the Airman's song—

Heinrich stepped onto the Mess Deck and halted, unsure of what to make of this unprecedented show of disrespect, and remained so until the near-twelve-minute rendering of the old Anglican hymn came to an end. After a brief silence, the audience erupted into applause and whistles, which is when someone finally shouted, *"Captain on the Mess!"*, prompting every man in the room to rise and salute, including the singing Airman, who slid off the tabletop and saluted with guitar still strapped over shoulder—

The ship's enormous Chief Security Officer, Lieutenant Commander Clancy Quorph, approached Captain von Schatt and saluted.

"Bring the Airman to the holding room," Heinrich ordered, "and send the guitar to the furnace."

"Aye, Captain," Quorph said, then pivoted 180° and stormed towards the perpetrator, the servicemen in his path breaking salutes and diving over tables to get out of the way of the hulking, scowling officer—

Down in the Security Office holding room, Airman Cash saluted Captain von Schatt upon his entrance, as he had been warned to do—

"At ease," Heinrich said, closing the door behind him. The room had no furniture, just four bare walls, a scuffed green linoleum floor, and a pair of buzzing fluorescent light tubes on the ceiling. "What is your name, Airman?"

"Airman John R. Cash, United States Air Force, sir."

"Airman Cash, who gave you authority to perform hymns on my Mess Deck?"

"Some of the guys asked me to play a song, sir. For morale, sir."

"And who gave them permission to request a hymn be performed on my Mess?"

"Back at Lackland they let me sing a couple of songs for the men in the Mess Hall every evening. I didn't realize it would be a problem here."

"Does this look like Lackland to you?"

"No, sir."

"What does it look like?"

"A ship, sir."

"Who's ship?"

"Your ship, sir."

"Correct. Two days in the Brig."

Lieutenant Commander Quorph escorted him out of the holding room and down the hall to the Brig, where there were three small cells, each furnished with wooden bench and brushed stainless steel toilet/sink.

Later that evening, exhausted but still too angry to sleep, trying to keep his mind occupied with thoughts of Vivian back in San Antonio, the young Airman could hold it in no longer. Lying back on the bench, he let out a full-throated roar and started kicking at the cell bars until the Security Officer on duty hurried in—

"Are you crazy, man?" the Officer asked. "Do you really want Captain Psycho comin' back down here?"

Airman Cash thought on it a moment. "I suppose not. Got anything to read?"

"We have a Bible."

"That'll do."

He settled back on the bench and ran his finger over the crackle-perforated texture cover and debossed gold letters of "HOLY BIBLE", then opened it randomly to James 4:7, to which someone had added a footnote in runny ink—

Submit yourselves, then, to God.
Resist the Devil*, and he will flee from you.

----

*von Schatt

⚓ ⚓ ⚓

On a dark and stormy night in June 1955, an eastbound Long Island Rail Road train slowed to a stop at the Lynbrook station. The doors slid open, and out stepped a stout old man clad in tattered black overcoat and bowler hat, in his mouth an extinguished cigar stub splayed at the end as if it had been struck by lightning.

Seeking shelter from the torrential rain, the man headed for the platform waiting room. Inside was humid with urine, a large puddle of it in the corner, to which he contributed. A homeless man was passed out on one of the benches, who did not stir while he peed.

Back outside, hands in overcoat pockets, he stood in the small space of shelter beneath the overhang of the waiting room roof, staring through the downpour at the brightly lit sign for the Spotted Toad Tavern, his left hand, sans pinky, resting against a soiled English-language edition of *The Lost World*, stashed within its pages a creased photograph of a smiling little girl behind a cash register, his right, minus index and middle fingers, palming a loaded Luger.

Like all good detectives, Torkel Nyström knew it was best to start in the public house. If von Schatt really did live in this village, someone in there would surely know of him. After a dozen years of sleuthing following the disappearance of his only remaining family members—Svea, Fjölner, and his beloved niece, Ingrid, whose voice he often heard calling for help in his opium visions—he was convinced that the girl had been kidnapped by von Schatt, and that, after catching his trail in Bremerhaven several weeks ago, he was on the verge of finally finding the monster.

He had never thought to look for him in Germany, with Hitler still in power when he and Ingrid disappeared, and the country in ruins in the years that followed. Then, one night several months ago at Oliver's—his preferred opium den in Södermalm, the Stockholm neighborhood where he lived in a low-rent boarding house with the other addicts—someone had left behind a copy of the *Stockholms-Tidningen* open to an article about how the Allies had turned post-War Bremerhaven into a major port in their effort to maintain peace in Europe, which mostly meant keeping an eye on the Soviets. At first he didn't think anything of it, but, as the black stuff worked its way into his recesses, the rusty old gears ground into motion—

He cut back his visits to Oliver's, going only every other night, until he had saved enough *kronor* to travel to Bremerhaven. He was surprised that the American seamen on the pier all knew of him, telling him that he was a Captain in the American Merchant Marine, and that his home port was the Brooklyn Army Terminal. Even more surprising, when he showed them the photo of Ingrid as a girl, they recognized her as von Schatt's wife, whom they had seen on the pier in Brooklyn, only now she was grown up and had three children of her own, a girl and twin boys, and they would all salute the arrivals and departures of the *USS Flatbush*.

He was directed back to the civilian pier to find a boat to Brooklyn. As he was leaving the Allied complex, someone called out in English, "Hey, oldtimer." It was a really old man seated behind a table with two mechanical devices atop it.

"You look like a man who appreciates modern technology," he said as Torkel approached.

"This is not so," Torkel said, also in English, holding up his hands to reveal his missing digits.

"I presume, then, that you would not be interested in purchasing one of these fine electric can openers. They were manufactured by the Third Reich. I found them at a bombed out factory in Schiffdorf. These are the last two."

"I have no use for such a device."

"Then, perhaps, can I interest you in something with a

little more firepower?"

"Firepower? What do you mean?"

The man rose and held open his overcoat just enough to reveal a Luger handle sticking out of an inside pocket—

"I scavenged it off a dead Nazi," he said. "It is still loaded."

Torkel raised an eyebrow—

"How much?" he asked.

At the civilian pier, Luger in overcoat pocket, Torkel booked passage on the *Alter Frachtera*, a clunky prewar German freighter, in a sixth class "cabin" that was actually a spare janitorial supply room that hadn't been used in years. The freighter made several stops before sputtering across the Atlantic to Red Hook, Brooklyn, where he found a longshoreman who knew of von Schatt and referred him to Krög's Butcher Shop in Cobble Hill.

There were no customers in the store. Behind the counter, on a stool, sat Axel Krög, staring off somewhere towards the far wall, when the dirty old Swede came in and asked about von Schatt—

"He owns two houses out on Long Island," Axel said in Swedish. "The one in Lynbrook, he lives in with his wife Ingrid, who used to live upstairs here. And there is another house in Valley Stream, where he has stashed my daughter, who also used to live upstairs, and who was still but a girl when he made her with child, when he already had a wife and child. And this being right after her mother died—my Hilda. He is an evil man. I have longed for the day that someone would come after him, but he is a protected man, by the Sicilian mafia, the Roman Catholic Church, and the American military."

"At this point," Torkel said, "I fear nothing."

The butcher gave him directions to the Atlantic Avenue

Terminal and instructions for getting to Lynbrook on the Long
Island Rail Road—and now, here he was at last, on the verge
of finally finding the monster, and saving his Ingrid—

The rain refused to let up. Eventually he went downstairs
and got drenched crossing Saperstein Plaza. The spotted Toad
was nearly empty, only a couple of businessmen in rumpled
suits slowly getting stoned on tonic and gin.

The bartender, Phil, raised a bushy eyebrow when the
soaked old man pushed his way in and dripped to the bar.

"What'll it be?" he asked.

"Vodka," the old man said.

"Vodka? What are you, a commie? Heh-heh, just kiddin'
pal. How 'bout a whiskey? That'll warm you up while you dry
off."

"Yes," Torkel said.

Phil put a shot glass and a quarter-full bottle of Old
Thompson on the bar.

"Do you know of a man named Captain von Schatt?"
Torkel asked.

Phil poured the shot and put the bottle back under the
bar.

"This one's on the house," he said, then, leaning in, "and
when you're finished, you're gonna get up and walk out the
same door you walked in. Understood?"

Torkel nodded and slowly sipped the shot, then placed
the empty glass back on the bar. Still drenched, but feeling
warmer, he headed back outside to the rain, where one of the
cabbies called out, "Hey, oldtimer, need a lift?"

Torkel got in.

"Where to, pal?" the driver asked, looking in the rearview
mirror.

"I am looking for a man named Captain Heinrich von

Schatt. I have been told he lives in this village. Do you know of him?"

"Yeah, I think I know the guy you're talking about. Big fella, white uniform, bright blue eyes, never takes a cab. I see him coming and going to the station with his wife and kids."

"Do you know where he lives? I am his long lost uncle, and I have come all the way from Sweden to see him."

"Wow, Sweden, huh?" the driver said, holding out his hand. "I think I can remember where the Captain lives, but I need a little something to jog my memory."

Torkel extracted an American dollar bill from what little was left of the currency he had exchanged back in Bremerhaven—

"Three," the driver said.

"Two," Torkel responded.

"Alright, two, since I'm in a good mood. I'm starting to recall that he lives in that crazy ship-house over on Hendrickson, near Dan's Foods. I'll take you there for another two bucks. Plus a buck tip. Non-negotiable."

During the ride, Torkel, as he had in so many of his opium dreams, visualized Fjölner and Svea finding Ingrid's note, which they brought to Sheriff Odinsson, who said there was little they could do about a runaway. Frustrated, they locked up the *Sex-Tio* and set out for Finland, taking a near-empty ferry from Stockholm, the only way to get there with Nordic Princess out of commission, 24 hours across the fog-shrouded Baltic. Finland, meanwhile, was fighting in the Continuation War to defend itself from being annexed by the Soviets, which had left Helsinki crawling with overzealous Red Army soldiers patrolling the *Ehrenströmintie*, most of whom had little tolerance for capitalism, religion, or Swedes asking for directions to the nearest convent—

"Fools!" the soldier exclaimed, vodka spittle spraying from his mouth and dangling from his chin. "Religion is the opium of the people!"

"We are looking for our daughter," Svea explained calmly, hoping this would have a calming effect on the soldier. "She has run away from Sweden and come to Finland to join a convent. We are only trying to take her away from the convent and bring her back home to Sweden."

Despite Svea's effort, the soldier only became more agitated, spewing spittle and invective about Sweden's weaknesses, and how someday she too would be under Soviet rule, and how he hated their stylish clothes and bicycles and those stupid little meatballs—

High above, Helsinki born-and-raised Captain Seppälälänennenn Jössänännämäläinen, navigating his Dutch-built Fokker C.X biplane bomber around the city's perimeter, spotted a Soviet Petlyakov Pe-2 coming straight at him and started firing his machine gun, one of the bullets striking the fuel tank and blowing the Soviet plane to bits over the *Stadi*, sending its Klimov 1,260 horsepower M-105PF engine screaming across the sky in a downward trajectory towards a Red Army soldier gesticulating wildly in front of a civilian couple on the *Ehrenströmintie*—

Torkel, during one of his routine visits south to Nynäshamn to stock up on canned goods and a little "pocket money", found the note on the door, now several days old, stating that they were closed indefinitely and had gone to Helsinki to look for their runaway daughter, and instructions to Ingrid if she returned.

"Runaway?" he said out loud to himself, his Holmesian instincts telling him that this did not sound right—his beloved Ingrid would not simply up and run away by herself, no matter how boring she thought Nynäshamn was—

After learning that the Nordic Princess Ferry-Ship Lines and its owner were no more, he followed Fjölner and Svea's trail up to Stockholm, then Helsinki. Upon his arrival in the Land of Sullen Joy, he sniffed out one of the last taverns in the city still open for business, *Mustikka Sammakko*—the infamous Blueberry Frog, where sailors rarely came to fisticuffs during disagreements but instead engaged in highly intense staring contests—and ordered one *lakka* after another until the bartender finally suggested he try the city morgue—which is where he ultimately found them, their bodies charred and disfigured beyond recognition except for the scar on a part of Svea's left ankle that was still intact, which Torkel knew had been the result of a sledding accident when she was ten with a boy named Ethelbert Frömor, her first crush, who, after the crash into the birch tree, would suffer the rest of his life with a bad limp and total impotence. The morgue attendant told Torkel that they and a Red Army soldier had been struck by the remains of a Soviet bomber shot down over the *Ehrenströmintie* near the harbor, but, until now, nobody knew who the man and woman were, or where they had come from—

"But there was no girl with them?" Torkel asked.

"No," the attendant said.

Torkel managed to find a sympathetic Catholic priest who telephoned every convent in the country, but was told by each that no such Swedish girl had showed up at their door. After accompanying Fjölner and Svea's remains back to Nynäshamn and being told by Sheriff Odinsson that they had no information regarding Ingrid, he arrived at the conclusion that von Schatt had taken her somewhere.

In the years that followed, he visited ports all over

Sweden asking seamen about von Schatt. While many had heard the name, none had ever seen him in person, and some thought he was just another evil myth like *Pippi Longstocking*.

As his body became more ravaged, Torkel lost hope of ever finding his little Ingrid, who by now would be a grown woman. The pursuit had kept him going, but now he was tired, and all he had left to look forward to was a hopefully painless passing, preferably at Oliver's. Somehow he managed to remain employed at the Stockholm Post Office, where he lost yet another finger to the sorting machine, his left pinky, and spent his meager wages on opium, still hearing the girl's cries for help in his visions, but they were far away and about to go silent, until he read the article in the *Tidningen* about postwar Bremerhaven—

On Hendrickson Avenue, the cab paid and driven away, Torkel walked the gangway to the front door. With his left index finger, he pressed the doorbell button and heard the bell ring inside. In his right overcoat pocket, he attempted to grip the Luger that he wasn't sure he could even shoot—

Down in the Officers' Lounge, Heinrich was browsing his new set of *Encyclopædia Britannicas* when the doorbell rang—

In the Heirs' Quarters, Walter sat up in bed, while Herman peeked out from under the blankets, where he'd been hiding from the thunder and lightning—

Upstairs, Heinrich, assuming that a caller at this late hour meant an urgent matter such as an emergency at the BAT that necessitated the newly-promoted Vice Admiral Arnold Houlihan to dispatch a Captain's Special Transport Vehicle, opened the door expecting to see a uniformed Merchant Marine driver on his gangway, but instead saw a short old man in a tattered overcoat and bowler hat. Thinking that the CSTV must be in use and that Houlihan had instead used one of the car services in Sunset Park—one of the lesser ones, apparently—Heinrich asked the dripping man, "What is the emergency?"

"Good evening, Captain von Schatt," Torkel said in English, surprised at not being recognized, considering that, on numerous occasions, he'd encountered von Schatt in the *Sex-Tio* and Ingrid had called him 'Uncle Torkel' right in front of the man. "There is an urgent matter I must discuss with you. May I come in?"

He was invited in and led through a small den, where there was a large painting of von Schatt on the wall, the blue eyes of which followed him across the room—

It wasn't until they had arrived in the bright, buzzing fluorescence of the Galley that Heinrich recognized the man.

"Uncle Torkel," he said.

"Where is she, von Schatt?" growled the old Swede, pulling Luger from pocket and pointing it at von Schatt's chest. "Where is my Ingrid? I know she's in this ship-house somewhere!"

"Fool! Hand over the weapon!"

"Where is she, *Captain*?"

In the Captain's Quarters, Ingrid was in a deep sleep, but her subconscious picked up the doorbell, then the familiar voice saying her name—

Heinrich reached for the Luger, but the old man found his grip and pulled the trigger. The bullet just missed Heinrich's left arm, but struck the two-horsepower motor of the electric can opener. A fountain of sparks erupted from its fatal wound, the device eventually settling into a prolonged death groan that would last several days. With a great roar, Heinrich again reached for the gun and this time knocked it away, then grabbed the old man by the upper arm and pulled him towards the door to the Lower Deck staircase—

At the bottom of the stairs, Walter, and now also Herman, watched the closed door up at the top, listening to the noises on the other side, until it opened and they saw Father clutching an old man by the arm. He shoved the man into the stairwell, beyond the reach of the staircase, and the man free-fell halfway down, until his shoulder hit one of the steps and he tumbled the rest of the way, landing at their feet.

There was a thud when the back of the man's head struck the linoleum. Then everything was still and quiet, save the buzzing of the lights from the Officers' Lounge, which Father turned off with the switch at the top of the stairs. His silhouette hovered in the rectangle of light until he closed the door, leaving the boys in the dark with the old man. During lightning flashes they could see his head resting in a pool of blood and a large gash in his crown, where a piece of skull had broken off and exposed his pulsing brain—

In the Galley, Heinrich picked up the telephone receiver and waited—

"Operator, who ya callin'?"

"Dispatch an ambulance to 6 Hendrickson Avenue in Lynbrook. A drunken old man has accidentally fallen down the stairs and is seriously injured."

While Father was on the phone, Walter ordered his brother back to bed, then retrieved his flashlight. Back outside their quarters with the door closed, he inspected the man's lifeless body and the pool of blood littered with skull fragments, rotted teeth, and a cigar stub, breathing in the scents as deep as he could, committing them to memory, until the doorbell rang—

Up in the Captain's Quarters, Ingrid stirred in her sleep, dreaming of being a little girl in Nynäshamn, standing on the pier at the ferry-ship terminal, clutching the Dala horse given her by Uncle Torkel, who was drowning in the middle of the harbor. She looked around for help, but the town was deserted, except for a blond-haired man in a white lab coat walking swiftly towards the train station. She tried calling to him but had lost her voice, and he soon disappeared onto a waiting train that promptly left the station. She then looked back out at the water, but Uncle Torkel was gone—

After the ambulance came and the medics took the man away, Father retrieved a mop and bucket from the Engine Room and swabbed the deck, then brought out the buffer machine and removed the film of mop water from the black linoleum, restoring its fluorescent gleam. After everything had been put away, he went up the stairs and again shut the lights, then went out the back door, the Volvo engine firing moments later and roaring off into the night—

Inspecting the scene, Walter was impressed to find no sign of what had just happened, save the lingering scents that would soon dissipate. He then started hearing a moaning sound, low at first but growing louder, which he thought was just the house settling, until Herman emerged from their quarters and started climbing the stairs—

"Where are you going?" Walter asked, but his brother didn't respond, continuing up to the Galley and out the back door. Walter followed, joining him in the dewy crabgrass, where together they watched the blinking red neon atop the shopping center monolith—DAN'S FOODS—D-A-N-'-S F-O-O-D-S—DAN'S FOODS / DAN'S FOODS / DAN'S FOODS—DAN'S FOODS DAN'S FOODS DAN'S FOODS DAN'S FOODS DAN'S FOODS DAN'S FOODS—

"What the hell is that moaning?" Walter asked.

"The Lava People," Herman answered.

"Who?"

"They're calling for Father."

"What the hell are you talking about, for Chrissake?"

"They're saying his name. *Hein-rich... Hein-rich...* Can't you hear them?"

"No, I just hear moaning."

They listened for several minutes, until the moans faded and Herman went back inside.

The older twin watched his brother disappear into the house, then went into the garage workshop, locking the door behind him—and that's when he saw them hanging on the pegboard, their shiny blades reflecting red from the neon glow coming in through the little window—handsaws, axes, knives, a ninja sword—

The moans grew louder, and this time he heard a name—

"Wall-terr... Wallll-terrrr... Wallllllll-terrrrrrrr..."

⚓   ⚓   ⚓

On the Saturday morning of Labor Day weekend 1955, Walter, now six and having graduated sucking tobacco pouches to smoking Winston cigarettes, set out for the stationery store to pick up a pack of smokes and the latest issue of *Swing Shift*, when he spotted, in front of the alley between Dan's Foods and The Law Office of Saul Rosenblatt, Esq., a boy and a girl sitting on the concrete, between them a wooden crate with "FREE KITTENS" written on its side in black crayon.

After purchasing his rations in the dingy store and emerging into the brilliant morning sunlight, he headed over.

Four of the kittens ignored him and continued playing among themselves. The fifth, trying to shrink behind the scrum, had terror in her big yellow-green eyes—

"I'll take that one," Walter said.

The boy, holding open a Dan's Foods brown paper grocery bag emblazoned with the store's "crown logo" in Pamplona red, felt a chill when the scary kid reached into the crate and snatched the kitten by her scruff, then dropped her in the bag—

"What will you name her?" the girl asked.

"What's your name?" Walter asked.

"Sally."

"Then I'll name her Sally."

The girl smiled.

Walter brought Sally the kitten into the garage workshop and locked the door. He placed the bag on the workbench and watched the rumples in the brown paper move around for a couple of minutes, then unrolled the top and pulled her out by the scruff. He held her in front of his face, watching the initial glimmer of hope in her big kitty eyes morph into feline terror. She started thrashing and managed to scratch his arm, which he liked, but his grip was too firm for any chance at escape. He cupped his free hand around her throat and squeezed until her body went limp.

An hour later, all that remained were parts, the legs and head sawed off with a hacksaw, the body skinned with a Norwegian scaling knife, and the innards wadded into four old cloth diapers placed neatly in the grocery bag. He would put the head and fur in the shoebox under his bed with the other heads and furs, the latter he used when humping the mattress.

After the workshop was clean and his new pieces packed away under his bed, he headed out, grocery bag in hand, down Hendrickson and across the asterisk intersection, from where he could see the boy and girl still sitting in the

shopping center with their crate. He turned right down South
Franklin, then made a slight left onto Lakeview Avenue,
heading east for half-mile until arriving at the Tanglewood
Preserve—seventeen acres of nature habitat with a large pond
stocked with goldfish that, in winter, was a popular ice
skating spot. The place was also crawling with lizards
wreaking havoc on the local ecosystem, this being three years
after the big pet shop truck crash on Peninsula Boulevard that
killed the bourbon-soaked driver and allowed the lizards
imported from Florida to escape into the preserve, where they
adapted to the harsh Northeast winters by retreating to the
tunnel far below that few humans knew of, the
Quoguepequacock Passage, a subterranean thoroughfare used
by the ancients that ran the length of Long Island from
Gowanus to Montauk, then continued beneath the ocean floor
to the northern edge of the Sohm Abyssal Plain and the Way
of the Grand Banks Arrow. The few humans who did know of
this passage treated them with respect during encounters
down there, which none of the humans on the surface had
ever done.

He followed the asphalt walkway through the crowded
recreation area facing the pond, where children were feeding
ducks and their parents sat on benches smoking. A group of
four boys had sliced the tail off a lizard and were now trying
to burn the creature alive with a tiny magnifying glass from a
box of Cracker Jack, but stopped and ran back to their mothers
when they saw him approaching. The walkway eventually
curved away from the pond, and he turned onto a footpath
that led back towards the water through a patch of woods. He
stopped at a secluded spot on the bank obstructed from view
in all directions by a small island in the middle of the pond
overgrown with bushes and vines.

After removing his socks and shoes and rolling up his pant cuffs, he waded into the warm, late-summer water up to his knees, where the bottom was covered with hand-sized rocks partially buried in the muck. Reaching down into the water, he moved several of the rocks, clearing a spot where he scooped out a hole. He went back to shore and retrieved the wadded diapers, then waded back in and placed them in the underwater hole as neatly as they had been in the grocery bag. He refilled the hole with muck and placed the rocks back on top, almost exactly as they had been. From the shore, socks and shoes back on feet, he took a moment to admire the scene, which showed no signs of disturbance. He went home and humped his new fur, his brief gratification even shorter than last time, followed by a long, aching boredom—

⚓ ⚓ ⚓

The only times Herman had ever seen his Daddy laugh were the rare occasions he was home on a Saturday night, when the entire family would adjourn to the Crew Lounge to watch *The Honeymooners*, featuring the hairbrained schemes of the Bus Captain, Ralph, and his pal, the sewer worker, Ed. He laughed whenever his Daddy laughed, looking back every so often at him seated next to Mother on the loveseat, Crowntainer in hand, exhaling clouds of Pall Mall smoke, fogging the tiny room, the boy breathing in as much as he could, unaware that he alone saw the human being in there.

Most of the time, Father wasn't home. Herman would longingly await his return, occupying himself by organizing his baseball cards, or sitting on the Crew Lounge floor in front of the television, as he was doing on a Saturday morning in early September 1956, watching *Captain Kangaroo*—the

Captain played by Lynbrook-born Bob Keeshan, who'd also played Clarabell the Clown on *Howdy Doody*—when the painting of Father started calling to him. He climbed up on the loveseat next to Mother, who didn't look at him, then on top of the backrest, reaching for Father in the canvas—

Seated at the Galley table, Walter, smoking a Winston with his orange juice and looking at the *Newsday* police blotter, heard something in the Crew Lounge that didn't sound right. He rushed in and found his brother standing on the backrest of the loveseat, face pressed against Father's painting—

"Herman, no!" he shouted.

"Daddy, come back!" Herman cried, the frame sliding along the wire on the back—

Walter leapt onto the loveseat and pulled Herman down. Together the brothers fell backwards to the floor, Herman landing on Walter, the painting landing flat on top of both, the canvas tearing into four triangular sections still attached to the frame.

For the next hour, Walter Scotch-taped the sections together on the back of the canvas in a Frankenstein-stitch pattern, but, on the front side, even in dim light, the seams formed a clearly visible "X"—

Father returned the following Friday evening. After adjourning to the Crew Lounge to give Mother her physical inspection, he saluted the painting, which is when he noticed—

Down in their quarters, the twins heard the bosun's whistle.

"Keep your mouth shut and let me do the talking," Walter ordered his underling. "Don't say a word except 'yes, sir' if addressed by Father. Got it?"

Herman nodded —

In the Crew Lounge, Ingrid, nude, and her three children, stood at attention, lined in foursquare formation, Male Heirs up front, females in the rear, facing the damaged painting, Heinrich standing aside to allow them a clear view —

"Who is going to explain what happened to my portraiture?" he asked.

"Sir, it was I, and I alone, sir, the First Male Heir, sir," Walter said. "I removed it from the wall and punched my fist through it, sir."

Walter, anticipating an eruption, or, at the very least, further interrogation, was disappointed when Father calmly ordered them to remain at attention, then pivoted out of the room —

Out in the garage, Heinrich gathered an assortment of tools and leftover building supplies — 2x4s, plywood, decoratively twisted wrought iron railing bars, cinder blocks, instant concrete mix, a spare door — and brought them down to the Engine Room, commencing four hours of wood sawing, iron clanging, nail hammering, and water running —

In the Crew Lounge, hearing the cacophony below, the children seated themselves on the floor, while their nude mother remained at attention saluting, blacked out on her feet. Four hours later, Father returned, covered with dust and streaks of concrete mix on his face —

"Females, dismissed," he said. "Male Heirs, report to the Engine Room."

In front of the space that had once housed the baby formula, now stood a floor-to-ceiling cinder block wall, in the middle of which was a door with "BRIG" painted on it, and an open padlock hanging from a hasp staple. On either side of the door were window spaces with bars of decoratively twisted wrought iron. Behind the wall was the cell, furnished with two beds made from a sheet of plywood sawed in half, each resting upon three-high stacks of cinder blocks at each corner. On the floor, against the rear wall, sat a metal bucket with the word "HEAD" painted on it, and, beside it, an unraveling roll of sea-green toilet paper.

Father lifted the padlock from the hasp staple.

"Both inside," he said. "Three days."

Walter went in first, followed by Herman. Father closed the door and locked it from the outside with the padlock. From each window, hands wrapped around wrought iron, they watched him pivot out of the Engine Room, then listened to his footsteps ascend the Lower Deck stairs and creak across the Galley floor on their way out the back door. Moments later, the Volvo fired and backed out of the driveway, then roared away into the Lynbrook night, both boys listening until they could no longer hear the motor revving in the distance, which is when the moaning began—

⚓　⚓　⚓

Alone at the Officer's Table, having just finished his SPAM and apple juice and about to enjoy his first mouthful of cherry crumb cobbler, First Officer Willis A. Streicher could no longer ignore the rising noise level on the Mess Deck, the Murmur given way to the buzz of 5,000 men in the presence of the most famous Army soldier in the world, Private Elvis Aaron Presley, whose brief but highly publicized military stint had thus far caused logistical flaps wherever he'd been stationed. Some of the other soldiers had concocted a ruse to get the King, who hadn't planned on singing during passage to Bremerhaven, to perform in something they were calling *"The*

USS Flatbush *Variety Revue"*, telling him it would improve the morale of the men, thousands of whom were soon chanting, *"Let's go El-vis!"*

Streicher stood and looked around for Lieutenant Commander Quorph, but, as usual, the dolt was nowhere to be seen, probably off in a dark corner somewhere chowing down a bucket of live squid. Knowing he could wait no longer before Captain Nutso heard the commotion, the First Officer knew it was up to him alone to put a stop to it, and headed into the dense crowd that had formed around the King —

"Excuse me, First Officer coming through," he said, but nobody paid him mind or allowed him to pass.

There was a huge cheer when Elvis finally agreed to perform, promptly followed by the bosun's whistle —

"God damnit!" Streicher exclaimed, but nobody heard him, all of the men now on their feet cheering as a volunteer piano player sat down at Sharky's old standup, and several tables were pushed aside to give the King an area to perform. The First Officer turned and headed for the kitchen and snatched two squares of cherry crumb cobbler, shoving both into his mouth at once and nearly choking on his way up to the Bridge —

Outside, the Atlantic appeared a sea of fire. The sun was setting behind the *Flatbush*, the brasswork reflecting the light and giving the Bridge a golden tint. This was September 1958, and Heinrich knew he was close, understanding now that it was not just location, but speed, timing, and a precise 180-degree arc that would commence upon turning north out of the eastbound shipping lane at Laurentian Cove and curving her back down through the southern-pointing tip of the Grand Banks Arrowhead, which she would have to pass through at precisely six knots or else the gateway would not appear and he would have to go back and start over —

As the *Flatbush* passed over, the vents on the floor three miles down puckered open, then shot a powerful lava stream up through the water, breaking the surface, fountaining high into the twilit sky —

Towards the end of the arc, Heinrich's keen ear picked up a cheering crowd, prompting him to blow his bosun's whistle —

When Streicher finally arrived, jacket lapel soiled with cobbler crumbs and cherry stains, the Captain roared, "What is this bluster on my Mess?"

"It's Private Presley, sir. The men can't contain their excitement. Letting him perform may be the only way to keep them calm, sir."

"Man the helm," von Schatt ordered. "I will handle this."

After he was gone, Streicher thought he had survived the encounter unscathed until he heard the moaning, then noticed the fountain of lava up ahead that they appeared headed straight for. Then, in his ear, a deep, raspy voice said his birth name, *"Willis Arnold Streicher"*, the hot onion breath giving him goose pimples —

Down in the Mess, Elvis was performing a high-flying version of "Jailhouse Rock", shaking his hips to the delight of his audience, morale on the *USS Flatbush* reaching an all-time high, more than a few of the men wetting their pants, others dancing shirtless on the tables swinging their uniform tops above their heads, until Captain von Schatt appeared at the doorway —

"Silence!" he roared, halting the *Revue*.

"Captain on the Mess!" someone shouted, prompting the men to stand and salute, including the shirtless ones on top of the tables, and Private Presley in his stage area. The now-

silent crowd parted as the Captain, followed by Lieutenant Commander Quorph and two Ship Security Officers, approached —

"Private Presley, I presume," said Heinrich, hands behind back.

"Uh, yes, sir," Elvis said, bemused.

"Private Presley, who gave you authorization to sing on my Mess?"

"The Colonel, sir."

"And which 'Colonel' would this be?"

"Colonel Parker, sir."

"And who gave this 'Colonel Parker' authorization to authorize you to sing on my Mess?"

"Uh, sir, I was just trying to entertain the men, you know, to improve morale, sir."

"You, a lowly private, took it upon yourself to improve the morale of 5,000 men on my ship?"

"Uh, yes, sir. I've played to lots of audiences larger than this, sir."

"And do you enjoy this 'jailhouse' you were raving about in song, Private Presley?"

"Uh, it's just a song I like to sing, sir."

"Since you like this 'jailhouse' so much, I am sure you will enjoy our Brig."

Heinrich turned to Quorph. "Three days. And have the piano sent to the furnace."

"Aye, Captain."

As the SSOs took the King's upper arms and escorted him away, Quorph unsheathed his two-handed melee sword and ordered the 5,000 men on the Mess Deck to sit and remain silent, every one of them complying instantly —

Upon returning to the Bridge, Heinrich found it

unmanned —

"Show yourself, First Officer Streicher!" he roared, but there was no answer. The moaning outside was louder than ever, and the ship, arc broken, was on a collision course with one of the fountains. Forgetting Streicher, he grabbed the helm and turned away just in time, but, when attempting to straighten her back out, realized he couldn't move, his body from the neck down frozen in place, his grip on the helm locking the ship in her turn —

"What is happening here?" he roared, then felt his throat being massaged by warm fingers belonging to someone standing behind him, which, at first, felt nice, until his trachea started burning, and he smelled onions —

"Streicher, is that you?" he asked, voice now weak.

The man laughed and stepped into view, clad in black silk robe with Asian dragon embroidery and garish red sash —

"Mr. Becker," Heinrich said hoarsely, "remove yourself from my Bridge at once —"

"Listen to you giving *me* orders," Mr. Becker laughed, stroking the underside of Heinrich's chin with his taloned index finger. "No need to get all jazzed up, *Kapitän*, my work here is already done. But I'll be seeing you again soon enough, and then you'll be *my* Captain. I have a nice big vessel waiting for you, and she's much more luxurious than this heap of scrap. Oh, and by the way, there's someone down there who's been *dying* to meet you. *Ta-ta!*"

Heinrich awoke on the floor with First Officer Streicher hovering over him. He attempted to push himself up, but his body did not respond per usual. When he did finally get to his feet, it took a moment to find his balance.

"Are you ill, sir?" Streicher asked.

"No," Heinrich said weakly. "Streicher dismissed."

After his First Officer was gone, Heinrich took the helm and turned the *Flatbush* sharply towards open water at full throttle, a maneuver that normally would have aroused him, but now he felt nothing—

Down in the Brig, the King, who, at the suggestion of the Colonel, had strapped himself with several cash belts, spent the next three days in private luxury, bribing the guards into bringing him bedding, pillows, pajamas, peanut butter & banana sandwiches, T-bone steaks, wieners, bacon-wrapped meatballs, Pepsi-Cola, cherry crumb cobbler, Dristan, Lucky Strike cigarettes, matches, a crusty issue of *Playboy*, a Bible, a six pack of Schlitz, and a rainbow of pills from Sick Bay—

⚓ ⚓ ⚓

Independence Day 1959, the twins' tenth birthday. Herman was outside with his Wiffle Ball bat pretending the backyard was the Polo Grounds, former home of his former favorite baseball team, the traitorous New York Giants, who, last year, along with the Dodgers, fled to California, leaving the great National League city of New York with only one team, the hated Yankees of the American League, the "junior circuit". Earlier, he had hit the ball into one of the gutters on the house, so he was now swinging at the little white moths fluttering around the yard and missing every time, until one landed on one of the four small rectangular windowpanes on the upper half of the door of the garage workshop. He swung the plastic yellow bat towards the window, pulverizing the moth and shattering the thin glass, the shards falling into the workshop, except for a triangular piece hanging from the top of the frame like a guillotine.

He looked around and, seeing no one else in their yard or

any of the adjoining yards, thought he was in the clear, until he heard a groan from inside the workshop. At first he assumed there was a small animal inside—he'd seen Walter bring all sorts of animals in there, bunnies, kittens, puppies, and, one time, a little baby—so he opened the door expecting to find some sort of creature, but, instead, found Father on the floor, on his side, body convulsing, eyes shut, face dark pink, forehead beaded with sweat, bloody spittle stringing from his mouth to the concrete floor—

Thinking Father had been wounded by the broken glass, Herman couldn't decide whether to run or go in and help, until Father said, "Get out," his voice not much more than a whisper—

Herman ran back into the house and down the stairs—

"I hurt Father!" he cried to Walter, who was on his bed looking at his magazines.

"What do you mean?"

"I broke the window on the workshop door! He's in there bleeding!"

Just then, they heard the main garage door slide open and the Volvo engine fire. They listened as the car slowly backed out of the driveway, then roared away.

"Come on," Walter said, leading his brother up the stairs and out to the workshop, where he quickly determined that whatever happened to Father was not Herman's doing—

"I don't know why he was bleeding, but it wasn't because of the glass," Walter explained. "The glass is nowhere near the blood, and there's no blood on the shards, just some moth dust. And there's only a couple of drops of blood on the floor anyway, so he couldn't be seriously hurt. And little pieces of this cheap glass wouldn't cause much harm, maybe a couple of cuts at most, but that's it."

Herman, still whimpering, stared at the blood —

"Relax, kid," Walter said, patting his brother on the shoulder. "I'll fix the window and clean up the mess. In a couple of hours, it'll look like nothing happened in here. Trust me."

⚓ ⚓ ⚓

The newly promoted Admiral Arnold Houlihan—who, despite the promotions, recognitions, ceremonies, bars, ribbons, cuff links, greeting cards, handwritten notes, kind words, pats on the back, and pay grade increases, still occupied the same office at the Bush Terminal, and was still responsible for the USS Flatbush and Captain Heinrich von Schatt, whom no one else wanted anything to do with—stood on the von Schatt family spot on Pier 3, lit a Camel, and stared out at the choppy gray Narrows. It was three days before Christmas, 1959, brutally cold, a cutting wind whipping off the Upper Bay, but, after the radiotelephone call he'd just received from the Flatbush, he had to get out of the office. The ship's Chief Medical Officer, Dr. Ernst Kopell, reported that von Schatt had fallen ill on the Bridge and had been taken to Sick Bay, and that command of the vessel has been transferred to First Officer Streicher, with their arrival in Brooklyn expected to be delayed ten hours —

A short time earlier, in the kitchen of the USS Flatbush, First Officer Willis A. Streicher felt the ship come to a full stop. He headed to the nearest observation post and discovered they were surrounded by lava fountains—he'd seen the lava plenty of times, but they weren't usually surrounded by them in this ritualistic manner, and von Schatt usually navigated past them without stopping—and couldn't decide whether to go up to the Bridge to see if something was wrong, or ride it out with a little extra cobbler. After ten minutes, oven mitt on hand toting a full tray fresh out of the oven, he knew something was wrong and headed up there, finding von Schatt unconscious on the floor bleeding from the mouth, a small pool of blood on the black linoleum beneath his chin. He called Sick Bay, and, moments later, Dr. Kopell, two medics, and two SSOs removed him from the Bridge on a stretcher, Kopell declaring him unfit and transferring command of the vessel to the First Officer. Fueled by cherry crumb cobbler, Captain Streicher spied an opening and pushed her to full throttle, the old lady battling the powerful swells for three hours before finally breaking out of the ring and returning to the westbound shipping lane—

Houlihan smoked several more Camels before heading back inside to make the dreaded call to the von Schatt household—

On Hendrickson Avenue, the Galley telephone rang and Ilsa answered—

"Good evening, this is Admiral Arnold Houlihan, US Merchant Marine. May I speak to Mrs. von Schatt?"

"This is she, *darling*."

Houlihan knew it was the daughter, but also knew the conversation would go more smoothly with her than with her mother—

"I have some unfortunate news," he said. "Captain von Schatt has fallen ill on the *Flatbush*. He is presently in Sick Bay, and the ship is now being navigated by the First Officer. We've already made arrangements to have an ambulance here at the pier when the ship arrives in order to get him to the hospital as soon as possible, but the situation has pushed back the scheduled arrival by ten hours."

"Oh, dear," Ilsa said, her mind aswirl with sudden possibilities that, only a moment ago, were far off in the future. "This is just awful, *darling*."

"He'll be taken to St. Albans Naval Hospital in Queens for further diagnosis and treatment. Some of the finest doctors in the United States Military are stationed there, and it is my sincere hope that they'll quickly diagnose and treat whatever the problem is."

"So awful, *darling*."

"Also, it may save you and the family some inconvenience if you didn't come out here to greet the *Flatbush*, as it's likely that Captain von Schatt won't even be conscious when they take him off the ship and put him in the ambulance."

"Thank you, *darling*."

After hanging up, Ilsa went into the Crew Lounge and turned off the television, then stood in front of the loveseat waving her hands in front of *Mor*'s face—

"*Mor, Mor, Mor*, it is Ilsa—"

"What is it, my love?" Ingrid asked, meeting her daughter's eyes for the first time in six months, when the gentleman in the bowtie was here with the papers that she and Ilsa signed—

"It is *Far*."

"Oh, dear! Is he here?" She looked around, ready to leap off the loveseat—

"No, no, *Mor*, he's still on the ship. The *Flatbush* has been delayed. *Far* is sick."

Ingrid's eyes sharpened.

"Sick?"

"They are going to take him to the hospital as soon as the *Flatbush* arrives, and there is a ten hour delay. Admiral Houlihan telephoned and said we don't have to greet him at the pier—"

"Of course we will greet him at the pier," Ingrid said.

"No, *Mor*, Admiral Houlihan said—"

"I do not care what he says!" she screamed, struggling to her feet—

"*Mor*, what is wrong?"

"We will greet him at the pier!" she roared, then stormed out of the Crew Lounge and into the Captain's Quarters, slamming the door behind her—

At the top of the Lower Deck stairs, Ilsa called Walter up to the Galley and gave him the news—

Moments later, in the Male Heirs' Quarters, where Herman was looking at the ads in the Nassau County Yellow Pages—

"Father is sick," Walter said. "They're gonna take him to the hospital when the ship arrives."

"And then the doctor will make him all better," Herman said, smiling confidently.

"It sounds like he's pretty sick. He might even die."

"Daddy will never die."

"What are you rambling about, for Chrissake?"

"Daddy will never die."

"Okay," Walter said, "but don't come crying to me when he croaks."

In her quarters, Ilsa went through the metal file box with *Far*'s papers to make sure everything was still there—bank statements, marriage license, birth certificates for she and the twins, and house titles, including the one in Valley Stream, which was in *Far*'s name only. She had previously showed these documents to her attorney, Mr. Rosenblatt from the shopping center, to verify there was no legal connection between *Far* and Wilma Krög, which he confirmed there was not.

Father-Dr. Panini had also confirmed that his only marital relation was to Ingrid von Schatt—

"In our *famiglia*," he explained, "we have a *Gumar Retirement and Relocation Program* that I would be happy to enroll the butcher girl and her children, at no cost to you, so they will be taken care of. They would be given a weekly cash envelope, private medical care, and a house far away in the swamps of Jersey—"

"No, *darling*. I want them out on the street."

In his office, Saul Rosenblatt, Esq. was shutting the lights, looking forward to sipping some blackberry brandy and smoking a fat Cuban while watching the fights on TV, when the telephone rang. It was Ilsa von Schatt, who, six months earlier, had him draw up paperwork to have her mother sign over power-of-attorney to her, and now she was saying her father was at death's door, and that he needed to write up a will for him to sign that would leave everything directly to her, and also make sure that the "tenants" in the Valley Stream house would be evicted the minute he was declared legally dead—

Later that evening, Herman was in the Crew Lounge when Father's scarred painting inspired him to make a "get well" card. He ripped a blank page from his loose leaf binder and retrieved the unopened box of Crayolas he'd had since kindergarten, then set to work. Not one to exhibit creativity beyond experimenting with different ways of organizing baseball cards, he folded the paper in the shape of a greeting card like the ones at the stationery store, then drew the ship-house on the cover, with giant flagpole in the green front yard, Old Glory up top, garage door open with brick red Volvo parked inside, Hendrickson Ave. street sign in the lower left corner, sky blue sky, lemon yellow sun—another beautiful day in Lynbrook USA. Looking back up at the painting, he was inspired again, opening the card and, landscape across fold, drawing the *USS Flatbush* navigating the choppy cadet blue Atlantic, above it another sky blue sky, this one including a big puffy white cloud with a message in black block letters:

DEAR FATHER, GET WELL SOON.

Knowing he had created a masterpiece that would surely get Father's attention, and, perhaps, even praise, Herman proudly held the card open and smiled. But he was also worried that, if Walter saw it, he might say something negative, so he decided to hide it until he had a chance to give it to Father—

Out in the garage workshop, Walter was browsing the shelf with the leftover paint and varnish from the house construction when his eyes landed on a small red and white can with **POISON** in red letters at the top with a skull and crossbones—**HOT FOOT MOUSE AND RAT KILLER**—the letters of "**HOT FOOT**" aflame, and a dead rat flat on its back with all four legs up in the air and tail in a death curl—*6 U.S. FL. OZ... 35¢... GUARANTEED TO KILL MICE AND RATS... ACTIVE INGREDIENTS: ARSENIC TRIOXIDE 2.6%, INERT INGREDIENTS 97.4%...*

"Perfect," Walter said, reaching for the can—

Late Thursday evening—Christmas Eve, after stockings had been hung with care all over southwestern Nassau County, but not at 6 Hendrickson Avenue—Ingrid and the children set out in the cold for the train station, and, nearly two hours later, arrived at their spot on Pier 3—

From his office at the Bush Terminal, an exhausted

Admiral Arnold Houlihan—wishing he was home in front of the hearth with Mildred, the children tucked away in bed, then, after making whoopee, he would adjourn to his study with a bottle of Jameson and his tumbler, where, in the leather chair next to the window, he would ruminate on the profound silence that falls upon the world on this Holy Night—watched through his Bausch & Lombs the von Schatt wife and children arrive at their spot and commence their prolonged salute, which, despite his strong suggestion to the girl that they remain home, he expected they would. The *Flatbush* was not scheduled to arrive for another two hours—*if* Streicher remained on schedule—and seeing them out there always made him feel awful, especially when it was cold like this, 12° with a wind chill of -20°, or on those hot summer days when their fair skin would boil red after two hours in the sun. Normally he knew it was best, for their own good, to leave them be—but tonight was different. He arranged for a Captain's Special Transport Vehicle to be fueled and warmed for midnight to take them home. He suspected Mrs. von Schatt might actually accept the offer, by which time, normal protocol will have already been broken—but, in case she did not, he was prepared to pull rank and remind her that even Captain von Schatt had to obey orders from the Admiral. He hoped it wouldn't come to that, but he didn't want them waiting for trains all night with hardly any running at this hour on Christmas Eve, and also didn't want them trying to go to St. Albans, where they wouldn't get to see him without the permission of Dr. Livingstein, who'd already been assigned to Captain von Schatt but wasn't scheduled to be there until 0900, after his morning schvitz.

He thought about calling the other family, whom he'd seen only once, on an afternoon he happened to be in Valley

Stream, finding Elmwood Street on his Texaco Nassau County road map, the address memorized because von Schatt had a small portion of each paycheck sent there. He parked and staked out the ship-house for nearly two hours, until the front door finally opened, and out stepped a woman, followed by a girl and a boy who looked very much like the regular von Schatt children. He was their Captain too, and they had no way of knowing that he'd fallen ill, and, if they didn't find out soon, they wouldn't have a chance to say good-bye—

Just after midnight, ten hours after the original arrival time, the lights of the *Flatbush* appeared around Bay Ridge Bend. As the tug was pushing her against the pier, Admiral Houlihan pivoted towards the von Schatts and joined them in their salute. Skeleton crews of office personnel on duty late on this holiday's eve began emerging from the buildings, uniformed Army, Navy, Air Force, Marines, Coast Guard, Merchant Marine, and even the civilian mess hall workers and janitorial crews, all forming a line that started with the von Schatts and Admiral Houlihan and extended halfway down the long pier. The ambulance waited next to the gangway with red light rotating silently on the roof, its glow pulsing against the *Flatbush* hull. A profound silence fell upon Brooklyn, and a bright, unfamiliar star appeared high in the night sky—

The ship's door popped open and an SSO emerged, guiding the front end of the gurney to which Heinrich was strapped, followed by one of the ship's medics at the back end, then Dr. Kopell. Slowly they rolled him down the gangway to the waiting ambulance, the back door already open, and slid him in.

Admiral Houlihan stepped forward and saluted the ambulance as it rolled away, until its taillights disappeared around the buildings. He then turned and faced the line.

"Thank you all for showing your support," he said, "and may Captain von Schatt be in your prayers on this Holy Night. God bless us, everyone."

As the crowd dispersed, Dr. Kopell approached Houlihan and said, "He's alive. Unconscious, but alive."

"How bad is he?"

"Bad. Off the record, I think it's the cancer. But they'll figure that out at St. Albans."

"Thanks, Ernst. Merry Christmas."

"You too, Admiral."

Houlihan took a deep breath of cold air and held it in his lungs as he pivoted back towards the waiting von Schatts—

"I have some encouraging news," he said, looking at Mrs. von Schatt, who appeared attentive. "Captain von Schatt is alive, and they are taking him to St. Albans. Unfortunately, we still don't know what's wrong, and you won't be able to see him tonight, but, in the morning, Dr. Livingstein, who is one of the best doctors they have over there, will examine him and figure out what is wrong. For now, though, I have arranged for a Captain's Special Transport Vehicle to take you back home, where you are to wait for a phone call from either myself or from someone at St. Albans. But nothing is going to happen until tomorrow, so I need you all to get home and get some rest. Dismissed, and Merry Christmas. God bless us, everyone."

He saluted them and they saluted back, with no objection from Mrs. von Schatt, as the CSTV, a black 1958 Continental Mark III, rolled up next to them. He pulled open the front passenger door for Mrs. von Schatt, then the back door for the children. After all passengers were in the car and the doors closed, he saluted the driver, Petty Officer O'Rourke, who saluted back. As the vehicle rolled away, he could see the good twin waving in the window, and he waved back, until the car turned off the pier and he could no longer see the boy. He lit a Camel and watched the taillights disappear around the buildings, then turned and looked up at the vacant Bridge of the *Flatbush*.

"End of an era," he said, taking a long drag and flicking the butt into the water, then heading back into the office to make one last telephone call before heading home—

By 11:00 the next morning, Christmas Day, the telephone had yet to ring, the only sound in the house the echo of the television in the Crew Lounge, where Mother was on the loveseat watching a rerun of *Truth or Consequences*, a game show hosted by former U.S. Navy fighter pilot Bob Barker—

Ingrid, seated in the studio audience at NBC Color City in Burbank, suspected that Uwe Carlsson was the person hidden in the sound booth operating "Beulah the Buzzer", which sounded when contestants didn't answer a question in time and had to face the consequences, such as jumping into a vat of strawberry Dream Whip dessert topping, or attempting to capture feral cats on Alameda Avenue to be spayed or neutered. The audience went bananas when the contestant was unable to answer the question, *"How many Dala horses are there in a dozen?"*, prompting a buzz from Beulah, and the curtain to open, revealing the consequence—Captain Heinrich von Schatt in his Captain's Whites, on his back, unconscious and bleeding from the mouth, a small pool of blood on the highly buffed black linoleum sound stage floor. Barker, holding his Radio Shack Realistic GSH1000 extra-long wand microphone, turned to Ingrid and said, *"Bob Barker saying goodbye, and hoping all your consequences are happy ones!"*

Finally, just before 1:00 pm, a nurse from St. Albans called and said to report to the hospital at 1600 hours to meet with

Dr. Livingstein, who would discuss Captain von Schatt's condition with them.

"He's still alive, *darling*?" Ilsa asked.

"Yes, Mrs. von Schatt."

"Alive enough to sign his name?"

"Dr. Livingstein will discuss his condition with you."

After hanging up with the nurse, Ilsa called Rosenblatt and told him they had to be at the hospital by 4:00, and that he'd better have the finished will with him ready for signing.

At 3:00, his Chiquita yellow '59 Cadillac Eldorado Biarritz pulled into the driveway.

"Are we taking your car, *darling*?" Ilsa asked from the front door.

"Only to the Lynbrook train station. I don't like driving this baby into Queens at night, and it's already getting dark. The hospital over there is right down the block from the train station."

The train stopped first at the Valley Stream station, then St. Albans. The brief ride gave Herman little chance to look out the window at the Christmas decorations on the houses and front lawns, some festive and gay, others religious and somber, trying to imagine what Christmas was like for the families who lived in these houses, wondering if the reason why Santa never stopped at their own house was because they didn't put up decorations—

At its peak, St. Albans Naval Hospital, built on a multi-building campus with an oval running track in the main courtyard and a lush lawn in the middle for outdoor exercise, housed nearly 5,000 patients from the end of World War II through the Korean Conflict. Now, during peacetime, there were less than 200. A modern marvel when it opened fifteen years ago, the weeds had long broken through the running track asphalt, and the place appeared headed towards institutional abandonment, a relic from the era before Dan's Foods and the bomb—

At the reception desk, Ilsa tapped the service bell, then, with an air, called out to no one in particular, "We're here to see Captain von Schatt, *darling*—"

They were sent to room 606, on the sixth floor. After stepping off the elevator and arriving at the only open door in the corridor, a tall, balding man in a white lab coat wandered out of the room looking at his clipboard—

"Dr. Livingstein, I presume?" Rosenblatt said, looking at the von Schatts for acknowledgment of his wit, but met with silence—

"If I had a nickel for every time I heard that one," Livingstein chuckled, extending his hand to Rosenblatt, who introduced himself as the family attorney, and was about to introduce Ingrid when he noticed her blank expression, prompting him to forgo introductions and explain in Livingstein's ear that Mrs. von Schatt was not feeling well today.

"Certainly understandable, Mr. Rosenblatt," Livingstein said, pulling a package of Chesterfields from the breast pocket of his lab coat and shaking a few loose. He offered one to Rosenblatt, who accepted, then to Ilsa and the boys—Herman shook his head, but Rosenblatt, Walter, and Ilsa accepted, the latter reaching into her Hermes "Grace Kelly" handbag to retrieve her Jaques Fath cigarette holder. Livingstein struck a match and lit Walter's cigarette, then Rosenblatt's, then Ilsa's, and finally his own, just as the flame on the stick was about to burn his fingers.

"Unfortunately," Livingstein said, exhaling, serious, "I'm afraid I have some not-so-good news regarding Captain von

Schatt. We have discovered a cancerous tumor on his larynx that has spread to his trachea. It appears that he's had this condition for a while, and that we are — well, too late. His body can't handle a major operation at this point, and it would only make the end excruciating for him. The tumor is obstructing most of the airway, so, to make him more comfortable, we performed a tracheotomy and cut a stoma — which is a small hole — in his throat just below it to enable him to breathe more easily, so he will no longer have to struggle to breathe through his mouth and nose trying to get the air past the tumor. He is awake at the moment, but it would be wise to say your good-byes now. I am very sorry."

"Can he sign his name, *darling*?" Ilsa asked.

"Possibly. At the moment, he's as high as a zeppelin with all the morphine we've got him on, but he may be able to."

"Can you sign as a witness, doc?" Rosenblatt asked.

"Certainly. Gotta get 'em while they're still warm, eh?"

After butts had been extinguished in the sand-filled ashtray near the elevator, Livingstein invited them into the room —

Face sunken, skin gray, blazing blue eyes reduced to flickers, Heinrich was looking out at the courtyard, the track oval still visible in the blood-orange dusk, when he heard them come in. He rolled his head and watched them fall into line beside the bed and salute —

"Oy vey," Rosenblatt mumbled.

Heinrich weakly lifted his right hand and, covering his stoma, spoke in less than a whisper —

"At ease," he said.

Walter looked at the intravenous bag attached to Father's arm, and at the medicine bottle on the tray beside the bed. Then he noticed the stoma, which he thought would be tiny and hardly visible, but the hole was the size of a nickel—

Herman struggled to untuck his undershirt and extract the card, the crayon wax sticking to his chest—

Ilsa watched Rosenblatt unwind the little red string on the manila envelope, then start patting his pockets—

"Ah, rat farts," he said. "I forgot my pen."

Dr. Livingstein extracted a black PROPERTY OF U.S. GOVERNMENT click-stic from his lab coat and handed it to the attorney.

"Thanks, doc," Rosenblatt said, then turned to von Schatt, but paused when he saw one of the twins handing him a homemade get-well card—

"I made this for you, Father," Herman said, staring into Daddy's blue eyes, which were looking back at him for the first time—

"Oy vey," Rosenblatt mumbled.

Heinrich took the card and briefly looked at the cover before opening it. He stared at the inside for ten or so seconds, then turned back to the boy.

"This card is vonderful," he said. "You have always been a good son, Rolfe."

Walter shot a quizzical glance at his brother, as Rosenblatt, wielding pen and papers, cut in—

"Captain von Schatt," the attorney said, "I apologize for bringing this up now, but it is vitally important for the welfare of your family that you sign your will. All you have to do is take this pen and sign next to the 'X'. Can you do that? Then I'll be out of your way—"

Rosenblatt felt the Captain's eyes fall upon him for a moment—

Wanting this man and these people to go away, Heinrich took the pen and signed, the signature itself not at all

202

resembling his formerly impeccable hand. Rosenblatt then handed paper and pen to Livingstein to sign on the *WITNESSED BY* line—

Ingrid stepped forward and looked into Heinrich's eyes. She saw not the current sick man, nor the man who married her, but the younger man who showed up at the *Sex-Tio* when she was a little girl and moved into the empty room down the hall—

"Good-bye, Captain von Schatt," she said.

Heinrich appeared as if about to say something, then shut his eyes—

There was a soft knock on the door.

"Ah, shit," Livingstein said, aware from his telephone conversation with Admiral Houlihan of the "delicate familial situation". He opened the door a crack and said, "Give me a minute," then closed it and asked Rosenblatt, "Are we ready?"

Rosenblatt, holding manila envelope strung shut with signed paperwork inside, answered, "I think so," then turned to Ilsa and asked, "Are we ready?"

"Yes, *darling*."

Livingstein opened the door and exited hastily, trying to both greet and obstruct from view the people waiting outside the room, a woman and two children standing at attention saluting—

Ingrid, recognizing Wilma, blacked out, but continued following Rosenblatt to the elevator—

Ilsa walked by with her nose in the air and didn't dare look directly at them—

Herman couldn't comprehend what he had just seen until he overheard his sister say to Mr. Rosenblatt, "That's *Far*'s other family." The boy was happy to learn that Father had another family, with a girl who looked like Ilsa, and a boy who looked like he and Walter, but wasn't sullen like Walter. Best of all was Other Mother, who was the most beautiful lady he'd ever seen. When she noticed him smiling at her, she looked at him and smiled back, which First Mother had never done—

Walter, lingering, stopped at the door when everyone else had gone and doubled back to his unconscious Father's bedside. He retrieved the Hot Foot from his coat pocket and twisted off the cap, then poured a perfect stream of the fluid into the stoma, emptying the can, which he re-capped and slipped back into his pocket. He waited a few seconds until Father's chest started convulsing, then walked casually out of the room, where he encountered another family with two children who looked like them. He slowed to take in the bewildering sight, then looked directly at the boy in the sailor suit, who became so frightened that he broke salute, wet himself, and hid behind his mother.

"Rolfe," Walter said under his breath—

An icy yuletide breeze greeted them up on the platform at the St. Albans train station. Rosenblatt headed towards the heated waiting room, while Ingrid, with Ilsa on her arm, took short steps down the platform, to where the front car of the train would stop. The boys followed Rosenblatt into the waiting room, where they were greeted by the tang of heated urine and the sight of a fat man in a soiled Santa suit passed out on one of the benches, novelty beard falling off and crusted with vomit, the tip of his grimy, uncircumcised penis sticking out from beneath his left leg—

"Oy vey," Rosenblatt said.

Train service was extra-limited on Christmas night, and nearly an hour had gone by when the door at the other end of the waiting room opened and the other family came in—

Wilma halted when she saw the twins and the old man at the other end of the room. For the next twenty minutes she remained in place, clutching her children, telling them to close their eyes, until the headlights of an eastbound train appeared in the darkness. She brought them back outside and down towards the end of the platform where Ingrid and Ilsa were waiting, but halted at the spot where the second car would stop—

Herman was looking out the window when the train stopped at the Valley Stream station. He saw the other family, who'd just disembarked from the second car, on the platform heading for the staircase, and Other Brother looked back towards the train.

"Rolfe," Herman said to himself—

The telephone was ringing when they got home. Ilsa helped *Mor* into one of the chairs at the Galley table, then picked up the receiver. They could all hear the woman's voice on the other end saying she was sorry to report that Captain von Schatt had passed, official time, 1806 hours, 25 December 1959—

"Thank you, *darling*," Ilsa said softly, before placing the receiver back on the cradle and looking at *Mor*.

"He is gone, *Mor*."

"I know, my love."

Ingrid rose from her chair and headed into the port side corridor, past the Crew Lounge, to the Captain's Quarters, disappearing into the dark room, the door closing gently behind her.

⚓   ⚓   ⚓

Captain Willis Arnold Streicher brought the *USS Flatbush* to full stop at *42°6'6.6"N 48°6'6.6"W—the* coordinates—where von Schatt's casket would be launched into His Eternal Waters. Admiral Arnold Houlihan was on board for this final steam of the *USS Flatbush*, having accompanied von Schatt's body—now embalmed and inside the casket, a Captain's White model with gleaming brass handles and brass anchor adornment on the lid—to his home port of Bremerhaven one last time, and now they were heading back to Brooklyn, stopping *here* for the burial at sea.

Before leaving New York, Houlihan had called both von Schatt residences to invite them to see their Captain off one last time, but no one ever answered in Lynbrook, and the Valley Stream number had been disconnected. He even sent Petty Officer O'Rourke out to the houses, but both were dark, save a television glow in one of the Lynbrook rooms, and nobody answered the doorbell at either. After von Schatt's burial at sea, the *Flatbush* would make her final homecoming to Pier 3, where there would be a brief ceremony with fire hoses spraying over the bow, and the Admiral slotted to say a few words, not only about von Schatt, but also the late Captain Jonas "Sharky" Waters, and her first skipper, Captain Richard Scully, who was still alive and running a crab shack down in Islamorada. She would be docked there for a week while crews removed equipment and supplies, then sent over to the Brooklyn Navy Yard for scrapping.

Streicher, in Formal Captain's Whites, left the Bridge and headed out to the Main Deck, where von Schatt's casket was draped in the Stars & Stripes. The normally ill-tempered winter Atlantic was placid as a vestal virgin, and there were no moans or lava fountains, only silence and pale winter daylight filtering through the sky thick with clouds, God sparing Himself from witnessing the spectacle.

Houlihan nodded to Lieutenant Commander Quorph, who ordered "Ready!" at the seven rifle-bearing seamen clad in Cracker Jack blues. In perfect unison, they removed their weapons from the safe position, then Quorph ordered "Aim!" and they pointed them at the sky. He waited several beats before finally giving the "Fire!" command, and seven shots cracked as one, their echo ripping through the distant silence, becoming fainter, but never going away completely. He then gave the second "Fire!" command, and seven more shots cracked.

Before the third and final round, four Merchant Marine officers removed the flag draping the casket and folded it into a triangle, then draped another one over it—Houlihan's idea, so he could present a casket-draped flag to each family. The Admiral then nodded to Quorph, who gave the third and final "Fire!" command, the bullets exploding from their weapons and hissing over the Atlantic for half-mile before diving below the surface.

The sealed casket, crafted from the finest Halifax oak, was wrapped in thick anchor chains and giant padlocks that would keep it weighted to the ocean floor. A dozen seamen lifted it onto a roller conveyer that extended beyond the starboard rail, and Admiral Houlihan nodded at the hand crank operator. The conveyer slowly tilted and the casket began moving, gaining momentum, chains thumping between conveyer wheels, before disappearing over the precipice. There was a brief silence, then a gentle splash—

For three miles the casket sank, slowing as the pressure increased, eventually touching down on a sandy knoll, where the light from above was no longer visible. It settled briefly, then the sand surrounding it started giving way and the box began to sink, submerging deep into the grains, funneling through a hole in the bedrock, and freefalling 126 miles through a blood-orange sky before smashing to bits on a charred pier set upon a sea of lava—

Naked, draped in anchor chains, surrounded by casket splinters, and fully erect for the first time in months, Heinrich freed himself from his restraints and pushed himself to his feet, then looked around until his blazing blue eyes landed on the vessel docked at the pier, an 883-foot Olympic-class ocean liner crudely welded together in the middle—

"This cannot be," he said, his regular voice having returned.

"Oh, but it is, my dear Heinrich, *it is*," said a gravelly voice in his ear.

"Mr. Becker," Heinrich said, turning to face the dragon-robed orphanage benefactor—

"What do you think of your new vessel, Captain?"

"What do you mean *your new vessel*?"

"How does this sound? Heinrich von Schatt, Captain of the *RMS Titanic*—"

"Admiral Houlihan will not be pleased if I arrive late to Brooklyn, nor will I. Send me back to the Bridge of the *Flatbush* at once, and return my Captain's Whites!"

"Oh, Heinrich, you're too funny. Do you really not know where you are?"

He looked at the ship. The lava sea bubbled. "This is a parlor trick," he said.

Mr. Becker laughed again. "Have you not ever wondered why she hasn't been found? I'm sure you'll be pleased to know that I had a giant brig installed with over 600 individual cells, so I can take my favorites with me on my travels, including one Captain Edward John Smith—well, he's not actually one of *my* favorites—he's kind of a bore, really, but this *is* his old ship, and he did take down fifteen-hundred innocents to get here—well, they weren't *all* innocents, but you know what I mean. Anyway, I know he's an old favorite of yours, and I certainly wouldn't let him navigate her again after his little mishap with the iceberg. Then there's old Adolf with that silly little mustache—such a temper—have I got a delicious story for you about that one, but I'll save it for when I introduce you to a certain lady who will be of great interest to you. All in good time, of which we have a limitless supply. And let's not forget about Wilhelm Klepp, a name you probably don't recognize—he's the man whose windpipe you crushed, and whose body you buried beneath the trash in that alley—that was a nice touch, by the way. Even your old Captain Hosenpinkel is in there, and he *is* one of my favorites—he doesn't even seem to mind being here, as long as he has his drink. But the Brig isn't even the best part—I've had the old lady repaired and upgraded by a team of Nazi engineers— best engineers ever, in my humble opinion. They fortified her with heat-resistant stainless steel and increased the engine horsepower from 46,000 to 166,000. She's also now fueled by the very lava she floats upon, so she can go on forever without having to stop and fill up. This baby can now reach a top speed of 66 knots—and you don't have to worry about icebergs down here, although you do have to keep an eye out for the giant diamonds floating about—"

"66 knots?" Heinrich asked, his erection intensifying and beginning to hurt.

"I see that I've whet your bosun's whistle," Mr. Becker chuckled. "Would you like to take her for a little spin?"

Heinrich looked up at the Bridge, his testicles aching—

"You know you want her, Captain—"

"Take me to the Bridge!"

Grinning, Mr. Becker raised his right hand above his head and snapped his fingers—

In the next instant, they were on the Bridge of the *RMS Titanic*, where Heinrich, still naked, found himself bent over the helm, arms positioned through the spokes, wrists tied together with his own white leather Captain's Belt—

"Becker!" he roared. "What is the meaning of this?"

Mr. Becker laughed and slipped out of his robe, revealing an erection even larger than Heinrich's—

"Why, Heinrich, you, of all people, should know what *this* is—it's time for your physical inspection, *darling*..."

⚓   ⚓   ⚓

On a sunny but frigid Friday afternoon in late January, the new 1960 Nassau County phone books arrived on Hendrickson Avenue, hand-delivered by a phone book delivery man from the New York Bell Telephone Company, who rang the doorbell at #6 but nobody answered, so he stuffed the two thick directories—the White Pages for the residential listings, and the Yellow Pages for businesses—between the storm and house doors, then hurried back to the warmth of his running phone book delivery truck—

As he had every January as far back as he could remember, Herman had been waiting for the new phone books to arrive, running home from school every afternoon through the Arctic air that had been hovering over the New York City metropolitan area for the past several weeks, only to be disappointed when they weren't there. But today they were, and he ran up the gangway and retrieved them from behind the storm door, then ran with them back down the gangway because the front door was always locked, around to the back of the house and down to his quarters, where he knew he would have a few hours to himself since Walter usually didn't come home until after dark.

He felt their smooth covers, then opened the Yellow Pages and breathed in the fresh ink on the golden pages until he became lightheaded. He looked up Island Gumshoe Investigations to see if they had updated their ad, and was disappointed that they hadn't. Several months earlier, he called the number and said nothing, until the gravelly voice on the other end said, "This call is being traced, kid, so I'm gonna find out where ya live and skin ya alive." He got scared and hung up and hadn't called back since, but started feeling the itch again after Father went away.

He usually made a run through the Yellow Pages first, but this time the little blue bell on the cover of the White Pages caught his eye and reminded him of his usual first task in this directory, finding their own listing—*von Schatt H, 6 Hendrickson Av Lynbrook, LY6-3963*—and on the line below, the only other von Schatt in Nassau County—*von Schatt H, 1 Elmwood St Vly Strm, VS5-0665*. He had seen the other *von Schatt H* listing for years, but most of the other names had multiple listings, so, until now, he'd never thought much of it.

On the Galley phone, he spun the numbers as fast as the rotary would allow, only to stop before the last one. A few seconds later, the switchboard operator got on the line and asked, *"Well, what are ya waitin' for? Are ya gonna dial the last number or what?"*

He slammed down the receiver, but got mad at himself and picked it right back up, this time dialing all seven numbers without pause, holding his breath as the lines were being connected, wondering what her voice would sound like, until the operator got back on and said the number had been disconnected. Thinking he may have dialed wrong, he tried several more times, until the operator exclaimed, *"Hey, what are ya doin', for Chrissake? I already told ya the number's been disconnected!"*

Back downstairs, teardrops falling on the open White Pages, he stared at their phone number, until, just to the left of it, the address caught his eye. Maybe they were still there. Maybe they just forgot to pay the phone bill. Or maybe they didn't need a phone anymore. Only a month ago, he had seen them disembark the train at Valley Stream. Of course they were still there. And, in the morning, after Walter left for wherever he went on Saturdays, he would take the train to Valley Stream and go live with them, and never set foot in Lynbrook again.

He pulled the shoebox containing his baseball cards out from under the bed and blew the dust off the lid, leaving in place the red postal rubber band holding it closed. He hadn't looked at the cards since the Giants left town, but he knew he would want them again when the new professional baseball league they'd been writing about in the papers finally started, the Continental League, an effort being spearheaded by the prominent lawyer Bill Shea, partner at Shea & Gould, that would have four new teams, one of which would be based in New York City starting in 1961. Maybe his new brother Rolfe liked baseball, and they could play Wiffle Ball together in the backyard, then afterwards do something naughty to earn them spankings from Other Mother.

Next he pulled the school books out of his army-green canvas knapsack and replaced them with pajamas, underwear, socks, trousers, dungarees, and undershirts. He didn't care about leaving behind the rest of his clothes since he had outgrown most of them anyway, and he knew Walter would notice if suddenly nothing was hanging out of the dresser drawers. After stashing the school books, shoebox, and knapsack under the bed, he went up to the Crew Lounge and watched *77 Sunset Strip*, then tried to get a good night's sleep, but was restless fantasizing about his new life, and Other Mother, until dawn's early light—

He slid out of bed, got dressed, and went upstairs to the Galley. The Saturday morning TV shows had yet to start, so he gathered bowl, spoon, milk, and box of Sugar Smacks, and placed everything on the table. After cereal and milk were poured, he sat with one hand shoveling it in with the spoon and spilling milk all over the gold-flaked formica, while his other hand held the cereal box tilted back so he could stare at Smaxey the Seal balancing a heaping bowl of heavily sugared puffed wheat on his nose.

After cleaning up—which he had been trained to do by Walter, who became cross whenever he found a mess at the table—he went into the Crew Lounge, just as his brother was coming up the stairs and the TV shows were starting, the first one a rerun of *Captain Kangaroo*. Herman listened as Walter began his Saturday morning routine—first he would sit at the Galley table drinking orange juice and smoking cigarettes while looking at the *Newsday*, then he would go downstairs and sit on the toilet pooping and smoking for twenty minutes, then he would leave for the day and not come back until after dark. Ilsa was rarely ever home, and never on weekends, while Mother, with the new TV in her room, now only got out of bed to go to the Galley or the head.

After Walter left, Herman waited fifteen minutes before

getting up and putting on his jacket and shoes. He went next door to the Captain's Quarters and, without knocking, opened the door. Mother was under the blankets, only her gray-haired head sticking out, her face inches from the television on the rickety brass stand next to the bed—

"Good-bye, First Mother," he said, then turned and headed out, gently closing the door behind him.

Heart racing, he retrieved knapsack and shoebox from under his bed, then set out upon the streets of Lynbrook. Instead of turning towards the shopping center, which they normally did when walking to the train station, he turned in the opposite direction, the way they went to school, then took side streets south towards Sunrise Highway. He maintained a swift, steady pace, looking over his shoulder every so often, until arriving at the intersection where Peninsula Boulevard awkwardly intersected Merrick Road, where he waited patiently before crossing both of the high-traffic thoroughfares. He cut through the empty courthouse parking lot to Saperstein Plaza, where the giant purple and yellow polka-dotted toad watched him bypass the ticket office and climb the 48 steps to the platform. He headed to the east end of the station, where the last car of a westbound train would stop, so he could look out the back window and watch Lynbrook disappear.

Not knowing if it would stop at Valley Stream, he boarded the next westbound train. He was relieved that the conductor wasn't in the car, and that there were only a few other passengers, all old men with their heads buried in newspapers who paid him no mind. He went to the window at the very back of the train and saw the rails behind them gleaming in the bright winter sun, and the Lynbrook skyline shrinking in the distance, the head of the purple toad, the top of the White Castle tower —

Two minutes later, the train rolled to a stop at Valley Stream. The doors slid open and he jumped over the gap onto the platform, then hurried down the 48 steps to the street, but stopped suddenly at the bottom when he realized he didn't know where to go next. He looked around, then went into the ticket office and asked the guy behind the window if he knew where Elmwood Street was.

"It's not far," the man said. "Just head down to the east end of the station to South Franklin, then make a right, and follow it across Sunrise until you get to Roosevelt. Then make a right on Roosevelt, go four blocks, and you'll hit Elmwood."

"Thanks, Mister!" Herman said, running for the door.

At the east end of the station, he arrived at South Franklin Avenue — Lynbrook too had a South Franklin Avenue, but not near the train station — then turned right and waited seemingly forever for the light to change on Sunrise Highway, which, even back home, he had never done. After crossing the six lanes, he continued down South Franklin, then turned right on Roosevelt, where the neighborhood suddenly felt different, the traffic noise from Sunrise now behind him, the street lined with telephone poles on one side and leafless winter trees on the other. He continued across Berkley, Cambridge, and Derby Streets, before arriving at Elmwood. At the corner, he looked left, where the street kept going forever, then right, which was a dead end bordering a park — and that's when he saw it, down at the end, his own ship-house, where, backed into the driveway, was a green and yellow Mayflower moving truck from which men in coveralls were removing things and bringing them up the gangway into the house —

He crossed to the opposite sidewalk and proceeded

towards the dead end, taking cover behind an Edsel Corsair parked in the driveway of the house directly across the street. He'd been watching the moving men for an hour when a teal '57 Chevy Bel-Air pulled up in front of the ship-house with a black family inside, a young couple up front and a girl and boy younger than he and Walter in the back, the man and the boy wearing suits, the woman and girl in Sunday dresses. They got out of the car and gathered on the sidewalk to take in the glorious scene before them, basking in the glow of the American dream, the man putting his arm around his smiling family—

"Home sweet ship-house," he said, then pointed up at the crisp new Stars and Stripes atop the flagpole and saluted. Mother and children followed his lead, and even the movers put down the furniture they were carrying and saluted, one of them humming "The Star-Spangled Banner", the others joining in—

"No..." Herman said, unaware that, behind him, the owner of the Edsel, a middle-aged white man with a drill sergeant flat-top and a Lucky Strike hanging from his lips, had emerged from his garage with a sledgehammer and a "FOR SALE" sign on a wooden stake—

"Say goodbye, son," the man said to the boy hiding behind his car. "There goes the neighborhood."

Startled, Herman took off running up the block towards Roosevelt Avenue—

"I don't blame ya, kid," the man said, watching the boy run for a moment, then pounding the stake into his frozen front lawn—

Shoebox tucked in the crook of his arm like Frank Gifford, overstuffed knapsack tightly strapped to his back, tears stinging his eyes, Herman ran as fast as he could, but tripped over a section of sidewalk that had been uplifted by a tree root. Stumbling forward, he tried to stay afoot, pulling it off for about ten yards or so, before fumbling the box and diving into the sparkling concrete —

Everything stopped. He looked at the blood seeping through the fresh white scrapes on his palms and inner wrists, then jumped to his feet, retrieving the shoebox from a strip of frost-stiff grass and continuing towards Roosevelt, no longer running, but walking as fast as he could —

"They're gone forever," he sobbed, navigating towards Sunrise Highway, tear streaks freezing on his cheeks. Back at the train station, he stopped in front of the bank of phone booths next to the platform staircase, where it occurred to him that maybe they just missed the cutoff when the new White Pages went to print, and maybe their new address and phone number would be in the 1961 edition — or, maybe, the operator might already have the new listing —

He ducked into one of the booths and picked up the receiver. The same operator as last night got on the line.

"I already told ya, kid, the Valley Stream listing has been disconnected, and I don't have any new or updated listings for 'von Schatt'. The only other active 'von Schatt' I have is on Hendrickson Avenue in Lynbrook. Maybe try again next week after the new and updateds come out, which is on Wednesdays, right after the morning cigarette break at 10:15. But now ya have to hang up, unless ya wanna make a call, in which case ya have to drop a dime in the box —"

He hung up and sank to the steel-plate floor. The quiet of the booth calmed him. He had always liked phone booths, not only because of Superman, but the way the heavy folding doors slid shut and silenced the outside world, and the doors themselves were cool, like the ones on school buses that the drivers pulled open and closed with the long handle.

In the quiet, he watched the people sitting at the lunch counter across the street—he had been counting on a home-cooked meal at his new house and had not made a backup plan for food, or anything else. He started feeling cold, and there was a heated waiting room right upstairs—maybe he could live here, at least until next Wednesday, when the new and updateds came out, and, in the meantime, he could work for meals by washing dishes at the lunch counter—

Upstairs, the waiting room was empty and warm. Like St. Albans, this one too smelled of pee, but he liked that smell. Down at the west end of the room, he took off his jacket and sat on the bench staring at the dried blood on his palms, then at the brick wall in front of him. He wished there were a television and refrigerator.

After five minutes, he was so bored that he took the rubber band off the shoebox and, for the first time since 1957, looked at his baseball cards. He had no enthusiasm for it, though, and longed to be back in the Crew Lounge, TV on, bowl of Sugar Smacks in front of him. He started yawning and dozed off a couple of times, only to wake with a start seconds later. He tried to stay awake but soon gave in, stretching out on the bench, using his knapsack as a pillow and jacket as a blanket—

In the sweet bliss of unconsciousness, Herman lost all sense of time and place as the afternoon rolled by. Passengers would come in for a few minutes, then leave when their train arrived, but no one bothered him. Outside, the orange winter sun was setting in the clear sky, just like it had when they went to see Father at the hospital, but Herman was dreaming of a summer's day at the Polo Grounds, clad in Giants home uniform, patrolling center field—in spring training, Willie

Mays had graciously agreed to move over to right field to make room for the young phenom, von Schatt, in center. Father was still alive and watching from a seat behind home plate, his Captain's Whites gleaming and clearly visible in the crowd, even from 400 feet away. Just before the game, team owner Horace Stoneham announced that the team was not moving to San Francisco, and that the Giants would play at the Polo Grounds forever. In the distant batter's box stood the Duke of Brooklyn, Edwin Donald Snider, who walloped one that Herman could tell was about to sail over his head. Like Mays in the '54 Series, he broke hard towards the warning track, his back to home plate, and looked up just in time to see the ball falling towards his outstretched glove—but, just as rawhide was about to strike leather, the rookie was awakened by the roar of a wild-eyed, long-bearded, missing-toothed hobo—

"Get out of my bed, you little bastard!"

Herman screamed and fell from the bench, then grabbed his belongings and ran for the door, not stopping until he was at the west end of the platform, where the last car of an eastbound train would stop. Minutes later, an eastbound arrived and he boarded, not considering that it may be a train running on the Far Rockaway branch, which had brown timetables and split from the main southern line east of Valley Stream, making stops at Gibson, Hewlett, Woodmere, Cedarhurst, Lawrence, Inwood, and Far Rockaway—but not Lynbrook.

The car was empty, the conductor nowhere in sight. After the train pulled out of the station, Herman felt the trucks beneath the carriage scraping against the guard rails at the turnout, and saw through the window the cars at the front of the train bending south. He started crying and became so upset that he didn't notice the train making the stops at Gibson, Hewlett, Woodmere, or Cedarhurst. Approaching Lawrence, the conductor finally came in and found the wailing, ticketless boy—

"Where you headed, son?" he asked.

"Lyn... brook..." Herman sobbed.

"This is the Far Rockaway train, kid. You should have changed at Valley Stream and boarded a Long Beach train, or one of the Babylon trains that stops at Lynbrook—"

Herman began to cry anew, even louder than before—

"Okay, kid, okay," the conductor said, fumbling with his belt, the coin dispenser full and tugging down his trousers, "we'll get you to Lynbrook—"

"I miss my daddy!"

"Don't worry, kid, we'll get you back to your daddy in Lynbrook. I'll even give you the tickets free of charge. But you're gonna have to get off at Lawrence, then catch the next train back to Valley Stream, then get off there and catch an eastbound Long Beach or Babylon train."

Herman continued wailing as the conductor punched the tickets he would need for the next two trains.

"Alright, kid," he said, handing them to Herman. "Just remember that when you get back to Valley Stream, make sure you get on an eastbound that's either going to Long Beach or Babylon. Do *not* get on a Far Rockaway train, or else you're gonna wind up right back here, and you'll have to do this all over again."

"O... kay..." Herman whimpered.

At the Lawrence station, the conductor, with brakeman's lantern and a small sledgehammer, signaled the engineer to hold the train while he escorted the boy off. The line was at grade here, the tracks embedded into the street crossing at

Lawrence Avenue, and there were two platforms, one for trains headed south towards the end of the line at Far Rockaway, and the other for trains headed back towards Valley Stream and west to the city.

He led the boy down the six steps at the end of the platform and around the pedestrian gates with the bells and flashing red lights, then across the two sets of embedded tracks and up the steps to the city-bound platform—

"The next train will be here in a few minutes," he said to Herman, who had finally stopped crying. "Get off at Valley Stream, then wait for the next eastbound that's not going to Far Rockaway. Got that?"

"Yes, sir," Herman said.

The conductor hurried back to his waiting train and signaled the engineer that he was ready to depart. Moments later, the air brakes released and the train pulled away, leaving Herman alone beneath a cone of dim platform light, shoebox in arm, knapsack on back, watching the red taillights disappear around the bend, just as the white headlights of a city-bound train appeared from the darkness—

This train was more crowded than the others he'd been on, men and women dressed up fancy heading into the city for the evening, the car thick with smoke. The conductor came through after Woodmere and punched his ticket, paying no mind that the passenger was a ten-year-old boy traveling alone—

At Valley Stream, he stepped back onto the platform he had seemingly just left, but didn't dare go near the waiting room. He stood in the cold for nearly twenty minutes, shivering, teeth chattering, until an eastbound train arrived. Despite the conductor's warning, he boarded without knowing where it was going, but he had to get out of the cold.

The train, though, rolled right past the Far Rockaway turnout, and, three minutes later, he was back in Lynbrook, nearly a mile from home.

Still shivering, he looked into one of the waiting room windows and saw that it was empty, so he went inside. He peed in the corner, then kneeled on the bench looking through the dirty glass across Saperstein Plaza, at the giant floodlit toad above the tavern door. Every so often, someone showed up and pulled the door open, releasing a cloud of smoke into the winter air. The taxis waited with their engines running, exhaust smoke shooting gray out of the tailpipes, then hovering over the empty street.

After ten minutes in the warmth, the shivering stopped. He set back out and headed for home, this time taking the usual route along Atlantic and Hempstead Avenues, the normally busy thoroughfares now deserted, his swift pace keeping him warm enough as a light snow began to fall. On the other side of Peninsula Boulevard, he started hearing the moans and could see the red glow of the Dan's Foods neon, the monolith invisible, the letters facing east and west indiscernible from this southern vantagepoint—

On the corner of Hendrickson Avenue, across the asterisk intersection from the shopping center, he once more had his familiar view of the red neon letters atop the west face of the monolith. Despite no longer being in motion, he felt warmer staring at the blinking letters, which would eventually become a single point of light, and one of the moans would distinguish itself from the others—

"*Herrrrrrrrrrmaaaaaaaaaaannnnnnnnnnnnnn...........*"

"Father," Herman said, wandering across the intersection into the shopping center parking lot, where the stores were all closed, except for the Best Great Wall. Leaving footprints in the thin layer of freshly fallen snow, he pivoted behind the building on the south side of the shopping center that housed Nelson's Barber Shop, Stella's Beauty Parlor, Guy John Jr.'s Men's Shoes Sales & Repair, and the U.S. Military Recruiting Station. He followed the road to the loading docks behind Dan's, the neon above lighting the area red like a photographer's dark room, giant snowflakes falling like ash —

To the side of the loading docks, near a pair of closed-lid dumpsters parked side-by-side against the twenty-foot-high brick wall of the supermarket building, was an iron ladder that led to the roof, but it only came halfway down the wall. Even with his unusually long arms and being tall for his age, the ladder, like the elusive regulation basketball rim, was too high for him to jump and reach. The edge of the dumpster nearest the ladder, though, appeared close enough to where, if he left his baseball cards and knapsack behind and got a good running start, he could probably leap from and reach the lowest rung. From the roof, he would be able to climb the iron rungs that had been permanently built into the brick of the monolith from bottom to top. The idea of climbing up there had always frightened him, but no longer, with Father's moans assuring him there was nothing to fear, and that, if he made it to the top, they would be together again, this time forever.

After years of hopping the chain link fence in the backyard to retrieve lost Wiffle Balls and other possessions, Herman had become a decent climber and was easily able to get on top of the dumpster nearest the ladder. From there, though, the jump looked much farther than it had from below, and he knew he would need a *super-fast* running start.

Giving himself as much runway as possible, he got his *super-fast* running start, but had not considered the layer of snow that had accumulated on the smooth dumpster cover. His feet slid out from under him, the back of his head hitting the edge of the dumpster as his body sailed over the side. He was unconscious before he hit the asphalt, landing on his back next to the knapsack and shoebox—

At the asterisk intersection, Walter spied the faint footprints in the snow that had mostly been covered by the continuing accumulation. Once on the trail, it was only a matter of moments before he was behind Dan's Foods, where he found his brother flat on his back next to the dumpsters—

"Herman!" he shouted, running to him, dropping to his knees. "Herman, wake up! Herman!"

Herman opened his eyes. Dark stars fell through the red glow. Father moaned.

"Father," he said weakly.

"No, Herman, it's me, Walter."

"Father," Herman repeated.

"Father's gone, Herman, and he ain't coming back."

"There," Herman said, attempting to point to the monolith towering above them, but unable to lift his arm—

"I need to get you out of here before you die, for Chrissake. Try sitting up, then I'll lift you over my shoulders."

Over the prior six months, Walter had developed a rigorous exercise program based on a collection of old Nassau County Police Department officer training manuals he'd found in the village library, and knew how to adjust Herman into a sitting position and lift him into a fireman's carry. After crouching to pick up the shoebox and knapsack, he transported the Second Male Heir and his cargo across the parking lot and asterisk intersection, back to Hendrickson Avenue—

As they headed up the driveway towards the garage,

Herman saw Father in his Captain's Whites standing in the sparkling snow saluting them. He tried telling Walter to stop but was unable to, and they continued across the patio, into the house—

Walter lay his brother down on the Crew Lounge loveseat, Father's blazing blue eyes above them watching from behind the "X" scarring his portraiture—

Made in the USA
Middletown, DE
23 October 2023

41112342R00137